Night of the
Red Horse

By Patricia Leitch and published by Catnip:

For Love of a Horse
A Devil to Ride
The Summer Riders
Night of the Red Horse
Gallop to the Hills
Horse in a Million

Night of the Red Horse

Patricia Leitch

Catnip

CATNIP BOOKS
Published by Catnip Publishing Ltd
14 Greville Street
London
EC1N 8SB

This edition published 2011

3 5 7 9 10 8 6 4 2

Text copyright © Patricia Leitch, 1978
The moral right of the author has been asserted.

Cover design by Chris Fraser
Cover photography by Karen Budkiewicz

A CIP catalogue record for this book is available from the British Library.

ISBN 978-1-84647-115-5

Printed in India

www.catnippublishing.co.uk

FOREWORD
by Lauren St John, author of *The White Giraffe*

For Love of a Horse, the first book in the *Jinny at Finmory* series, is my favourite pony book of all time. I read it for the first time when I was about eleven and every bit as horse mad as Jinny, and it's hard to overstate how much impact it had on me and how much I related to the story and to Jinny's relationship with her horse. It didn't matter that Jinny lived at Finmory on the Scottish moors and spent her days passionately trying to save or tame a chestnut Arab mare, and I lived on a remote farm in Africa and spent my days trying to save and train a black stallion, it seemed to me that the way we thought, felt and dreamed about the horses we loved was identical.

Imagine having a best friend who thinks about riding exactly the way you do; who gets into the same kind of disastrous, scary or embarrassing situations and suffers the same kind of highs and lows, and who just happens to have the horse of your dreams. That's what Jinny and Shantih were for me. Over the years, scores of other fans of the series have felt the same way. You will too. And if you're anything like me, you'll be drawing pictures of Shantih and pinning them up on your bedroom wall, reading each book at least five times, and wishing and dreaming that you had a chestnut Arab mare just like Shantih and could gallop across the moors with Jinny, mysterious, magical Ken, and all the other characters who make up Jinny's world at Finmory.

You're in for the ride of your life. Enjoy!

Lauren St John
London, 2010

One

'Again,' said Jinny Manders. 'I'm going round again.'

Shantih, the chestnut Arab Jinny was riding, pranced impatiently, threatening to buck – her white stockings glinting in the grey evening, her red-gold coat bright. A wind gusted in from the sea, blowing back Jinny's long, red hair and fanning out her horse's mane and tail.

'Isn't it getting rather late?' said Sue Horton. 'Mum will be wondering what's happened to me.'

She glanced over her shoulder to where the Horton's yellow tent perched on the grass above Finmory Bay. Sue and her parents were spending their summer holidays camping at Finmory. At the last minute they had managed to borrow a trailer and bring Pippen, Sue's skewbald pony, on holiday with them. Now he stood, four-square and solid, his feet planted firmly on the ground and an expression of mild disapproval at the Arab's behaviour on his brown and white face. His rider was as square and sturdy as her pony. She was twelve years old, the same age as Jinny, with short brown hair, hazel eyes and an open expression.

'You've jumped her round four times already,' said Sue. 'You'll only sicken her.'

'Not over these silly little jumps,' stated Jinny, and before Sue could produce any more of her common-sense arguments Jinny had eased her hold on Shantih's reins, tightened her legs against her horse's sides and they were away, galloping at the first jump.

Shantih thundered up to the first pole. Yards in front of it she launched herself into the air and sailed over it in a wide, flowing arc. Jinny, sitting tight in the saddle, moved with her horse. A grin of sheer delight spread over her face as Shantih, gathering speed, flew on down the field, over the jump made from one of Mr MacKenzie's cast-out sheep pens and over the third jump of two straw bales.

Turning to come back up the field, Shantih was going faster than ever. Her speed whipped tears from Jinny's eyes, made her laugh aloud. She could have gone on galloping and jumping Shantih forever. It was more exciting than anything she had ever known in all her life.

The last of the five jumps was made of wooden fish boxes piled precariously on top of each other. Shantih was galloping too fast to be able to time her take-off and Jinny knew nothing about such things. She only knew that, most of the time, all she needed to do was to sit on Shantih and her horse would jump anything. But this time Shantih took off too soon. Her front feet sent the boxes flying, and in a sudden panic Shantih was bolting round the field, her head low, her body tight and her hooves beating out a frenzied tattoo of fear.

It took Jinny four circles of the field before she was in control again.

'Well, surely that's enough,' said Sue, as Jinny brought Shantih from a trot to a walk and rode her back to Pippen. 'I told you she had had enough.'

'Enough! Shantih would go on jumping all night. It's these silly jumps. If we had proper ones . . .'

'If that last jump had been fixed she would have fallen. Coming at it at that speed! Just stupid. You let her go too fast.'

'I like her fast,' said Jinny irritably.

Although Sue arriving with Pippen and lending her a saddle had been the best thing that could possibly have happened in Jinny's summer holidays, she couldn't help feeling that at times Sue was depressingly right.

Almost as bad as Petra, Jinny thought. *As if an elder sister isn't enough*. She sighed gustily.

'I'm going in anyway,' decided Sue.

Reluctantly, Jinny followed her out of the field.

'Tomorrow,' said Jinny, 'we'll build some proper jumps.'

'OK,' said Sue, grinning, and instantly Jinny was sorry that she had even thought that Sue was in the least like Petra.

'See you tomorrow about ten,' Jinny called back, as Sue took Pippen to their tent to give him a feed before she turned him out for the night in Mr MacKenzie's field.

Jinny rode Shantih back across the fields to Finmory. The Arab walked out with her long-reaching stride. She was still excited after her gallop. Her neck was arched, her ears alert and her eyes wide to catch the least movement on the moorland that stretched about her, grey and barren in the late summer evening.

Lights shone from the windows of Finmory House, glowing warm and welcoming.

Home, thought Jinny, and shivered with pleasure to think that home wasn't a flat in the city as it had been a year ago when the Manders family had lived in Stopton. Now, home was Finmory House, a grey stone house in the north of Scotland, standing between mountains and sea and surrounded by heather-clad moors. The only other house that Jinny could see was Mr MacKenzie's farm, and beyond that it was miles to Glenbost village. Jinny loved it all – the space, the freedom and the silence.

In Stopton, Mr Manders had been a probation officer. Now he was a potter, selling his pots to Nell Storr's craft shop in Inverburgh, and the author of a book about the slums of Stopton and the lives of the people there with whom he had worked. *Almost an author*, thought Jinny more truthfully. Her father had written the book and one publisher had turned it down but he had sent it to another. So far he had not heard whether they wanted to publish it or not.

Petra, Jinny's elder sister, was fifteen. Riding home, Jinny knew exactly what Petra would be doing. She would be playing the piano, practising the pieces for her music examination. Jinny could picture her, sitting very straight on the piano stool, wearing neat, smart clothes, for everything that Petra wore became neat and smart the second she put it on. She would be playing very precisely, her face concentrating on getting each and every note exactly right – as each and every hair of Petra's dark, short curls was always exactly right.

We're not sisters, thought Jinny. *I'm a changeling. Petra couldn't possibly be my sister. At least I won't have to go to the same school as her, where they would always be telling me how wonderful Petra is.*

Until now, Jinny had gone to the village school in Glenbost, riding there with Mike, her ten-year-old brother, on Punch and Bramble, two Highland ponies borrowed in the off season from Miss Tuke's trekking centre, and Petra had been a weekly boarder at Duninver Grammar School. When they all returned to school in September, Petra would go back to Duninver, but Jinny was to travel each day by school bus to the new comprehensive school at Inverburgh. It had been like a miracle when Jinny had heard that they were building a new school and that she would be able to travel there each day. She could not possibly have left Shantih at Finmory; could not possibly have gone to stay at the Duninver school hostel.

'I just wouldn't have gone and that would have been that.' Jinny laid her hand on Shantih's warm, strong neck. 'I couldn't have left you alone all week, could I?'

Shantih flickered her ears at the sound of Jinny's voice and flurried her nostrils in reply to the question.

Warm and sweet and sudden, love for Shantih filled Jinny. Once the Arab had been 'Yasmin the Killer Horse', beaten into a fury in a circus. Jinny had rescued her, made Shantih her own, tamed and gentled her.

'And now you can jump,' said Jinny, 'I must go on schooling you.'

Jinny knew that Sue didn't consider what she had been doing on Shantih tonight as schooling, but then Sue only had Pippen. She didn't know what it was like to jump Shantih, to feel as if you had wings, so that all you wanted to do was to go on jumping, faster and higher, over and over again.

Jinny rode up to the stables at Finmory House. Once they had been broken-down, deserted outhouses, but now they were a feed house, tack room, two stalls that Punch and Bramble used, and a loose box for Shantih.

Mike was waiting for her.

'Where have you been?' he asked, opening the loose-box door for Jinny. 'You've been ages. They've been waiting for you since before tea.'

Mike had short curly hair like Petra's and brown eyes. Jinny liked her brother. Even if he hadn't been related to her, Jinny thought, she would have wanted to know him. He was easy to be with, not moody, always the same.

'Who?' Jinny asked, taking off Shantih's tack.

'Two people,' said Mike. 'Especially to see you. So buck up.'

'Who?' said Jinny again, but Mike had gone. *Well, whoever they are they'll have to wait until I've finished with Shantih*, she thought.

Jinny tipped oats and nuts into the trough and stood watching Shantih eating her feed. When the horse had chased the last elusive grain of corn into the corner of her trough and swallowed it down, Jinny put on her halter and led her down to her field.

Punch and Bramble were at Miss Tuke's being trekking ponies again, so Shantih was alone. Jinny had thought that Pippen could have shared Shantih's field, but Mr MacKenzie had said the Manders' grass needed resting and Pippen would be better in his field.

'I expect the Hortons are paying Mr MacKenzie for their grazing,' Mr Manders had suggested, and Jinny had agreed that it was more than likely.

Shantih waited while Jinny gave her a sugar lump, then plunged away from her. She lay down to roll, her legs suddenly clumsy and ridiculous as she scrubbed herself into the grass. She surged upright again and instantly began to graze. For a moment longer Jinny leaned on the gate, watching her, hearing her cropping the grass and, in the distance, the slow rhythm of the waves in the bay.

'Dear horse,' said Jinny and walked backwards up the path until Shantih's gold was only a grey silhouette in the grey evening.

People to see me, Jinny thought, and she spun round and began to run up to the house, imagining that the committee who chose the showjumping team for the Olympic Games were waiting to see her.

'Of course, we do realise that you are not quite ready yet, but we like to select promising partnerships of horse and rider and start training them together for a few years before they actually compete in the Games. Can't guarantee you a place in the team, of course, but from what we've seen of your horse we think you've a pretty decent chance.'

The sight of an unknown Land Rover parked in front of Finmory brought Jinny back to reality. There really was someone in the house waiting to see her. Jinny had thought that Mike was only kidding her, wanting her to hurry up so that she would be in time to dry the dishes.

A loud woman's voice came from an open window.

'These Scottish digs can be rather amusing, but of course when Terry was alive, most of our work was in Egypt.'

Jinny didn't know the voice. It didn't sound like someone who would want to see her. Cautiously she went round to the side of the house and in by the back door.

Ken was standing by the sink, washing some stones he had collected from the beach. He had put the stones in a basin of water and was gazing down at them, meditating on them.

Ken Dawson lived with the Manders. He worked with Mr Manders in the pottery, cared for the vegetable garden, which he had created and which fed them all with vegetables and fruit. 'No need for all the slaughtering. The earth feeds us, if we'll only let it,' Ken said. And with Ken to look after the garden it did.

Ken was eighteen – tall, bony, with straw-coloured hair growing long, past his shoulders, his green eyes calm in his weather-beaten face. Ken had saved Jinny's life and had helped her to rescue Shantih.

Mr Manders had been Ken's probation officer in Stopton when Ken had been involved in a break-in to a warehouse. On the last day of his probation Ken had said to Mr Manders, 'I'd nothing to do with it.' 'I know,' Mr Manders had acknowledged.

After the Manders had come to live at Finmory,

Ken had arrived with Kelly, his grey, shaggy, yellow-eyed dog, and offered to help. Now he was part of the family. *Just as well he found us*, Jinny often thought. *Just as well for all of us.* For Ken's rich parents wanted nothing to do with him. They sent him a monthly cheque through their bank. 'So that they'll know I'm not starving,' Ken said.

'Who's here?' Jinny asked, going across the kitchen to look at Ken's stones.

He handed one to her, holding it carefully between bony forefinger and thumb.

'A flint,' he said. 'You can see where it was chipped to make a sharp edge on it. Made in the Stone Age and now you're holding it.' He laid it reverently on Jinny's open palm.

'I thought I heard you come in,' exclaimed Jinny's mother, bursting into the kitchen. 'Where have you been?'

Jinny gave the flint back to Ken. She knew from the tone of her mother's voice that things more urgent than Ken's stones were about to overtake her.

'Jumping Shantih,' Jinny replied, while Ken turned himself off from their raised voices and went on staring silently down at his underwater, shimmering stones.

'All afternoon and all evening?' said Mrs Manders in obvious disbelief.

'Well, more or less,' said Jinny, trying to remember anything else she might have done.

But her mother wasn't really wanting to know.

'You've to go upstairs straight away and tidy your bedroom. It's an absolute disgrace.'

'Now?' asked Jinny in amazement. Remembering the strewn clothes, books, paints, paper and all the other things that were rioting over her bedroom floor, Jinny could quite see why her mother should think that it needed tidying up, but she couldn't imagine why she wanted her to do it now.

'This very minute. Two archaeologists arrived hours ago wanting to see your mural. Luckily, before I took them upstairs, I had the sense to look at your room. It is a shambles, Jinny. I wasn't going to clear it up after you so I told them they would have to wait until you came home. We're all onto our fourth coffee, so do you think you could hurry up?'

'I don't see why they should get into my bedroom . . .' began Jinny.

'At once,' said her mother in the voice which Jinny didn't argue with.

Jinny raced up the wide flight of stairs, ran along the landing corridor to where an almost vertical ladder of stairs led up to her room.

When she had first seen it, Jinny had known that this must be her room at Finmory. It was divided into two parts by an archway. The window on the left looked out to sea – down over Finmory's wild garden to the ponies' field and on to Finmory Bay. Waking in the morning, Jinny would lean out and call Shantih's name, and her horse would look up and whinny in reply. The opposite window looked out over the moors and the high, rocky crags hustling up against the sky. It was in this half of the room that there was a painting on the wall which the archaeologists wanted to see. A mural of a red horse with yellow eyes that came charging through a growth of blue-green forest branches laden with white blooms.

Jinny could see what her mother had meant about her room. It was worse than usual. She gathered up armfuls of clothes and pushed them into drawers, stacked books into piles, collected pencils, felt-tipped pens, pastels and paints into boxes and tried to sort out the sheets of paper that lay like autumn leaves after a gale, covering everything.

The walls, too, were covered with Jinny's pictures – drawings, paintings, collages. They were mostly of Shantih and the animals that Jinny had seen on the moors – red deer, foxes, eagles, and the insects that lived their intense, secret lives in the same world as blind, gigantic humans.

Suddenly Jinny stopped clearing up. If the unknown archaeologists came up to her room they would see her pictures on the walls and Jinny hated anyone looking at her drawings. She wondered if she should make a fuss, go down and tell them that her bedroom was private.

'Jinny,' called her mother, still using 'that' voice, 'are you ready? Can we come up?'

Jinny pushed a last pile of drawings under the bed, captured a stray sock and hid it beneath her bedclothes and glanced quickly around. Her room was not perfect but it would have to do.

'Yes, OK,' she called down, and waited, hearing footsteps and voices growing louder as they approached.

Jinny's mother came in first, looking round quickly to see if Jinny's tidying was satisfactory. She was followed by a large woman in a tweed suit, bulletproof stockings and sturdy lace-up shoes. Her white hair was cropped, her wrinkled skin a dusty yellow. A young man with pimples and thick glasses peered out from her shadow.

'This is Jinny,' said Mrs Manders. 'Jinny, this is Mrs Horgan.'

'Freda,' said the woman, holding out a powerful hand to Jinny.

Jinny grasped it, said how do you do – but already Freda was striding towards the mural.

'And Ronald,' said Mrs Manders, but the young man was trotting behind Freda, paying no attention to Jinny.

They both stood for a moment in front of the Red Horse, their heads thrust forward staring at it, then Freda gave a snort of disgust.

'Useless,' she announced. 'Totally useless. Obviously

painted this century. Crude primitive.'

'Waste of an afternoon,' agreed Ronald. 'No chance of an original underneath.' And he scratched at the paint with his fingernail.

'Well, I like it,' protested Jinny indignantly. 'I like it very much indeed.'

Secretly, Jinny was afraid of the Horse. There was a strangeness about it, a power. When Shantih had been trapped in a circus, and Jinny had thought she would never see her again, she had drawn a picture of the Arab galloping free on the Finmory moors and pinned it on the wall opposite the Red Horse, and Shantih had come to Finmory. Jinny didn't really believe that the Red Horse could have had anything to do with bringing Shantih here, but then you never knew for certain about these things. You could never be quite sure about them.

'And it's mine,' added Jinny, as if that settled the whole matter.

'Jinny,' warned her mother.

'Now please don't get the wrong idea. I'm sure you're very fond of the old fellow, but we're looking for something else. Traces of a pony cult that we think might have existed in these parts. The Celts had many sacred animals – the horse, the stag, the dog, the boar and several others are all linked up with Celtic mythology. We're excavating a Celtic settlement at Brachan, about twelve miles from here. One of the locals told us there was an old painting of a horse at

Finmory House. We pricked up our ears when we heard that. There's cup-and-ball markings on some of the rocks about Finmory. Wouldn't mind excavating here sometime. Definite links with the Celts. So we took a chance and came over. Decent of you to let us see it, but no interest.'

'What's a pony cult?' asked Jinny.

'The Celts worshipped the Earth Mother, and one of the forms she took was the goddess Epona, goddess of ponies and foals. Not so long ago, about the turn of the century, a statuette of Epona was found quite close to where we're digging. A tinker found it, handed it into a museum in Inverburgh. Still there. Utterly ludicrous, a museum that size sitting on a valuable piece like that. Ought to be in London.'

'I didn't see it,' said Jinny. She had been to Inverburgh Museum with her teacher, Miss Broughton, and the other pupils at Glenbost School. 'I was doing a project on horses and I'm sure Miss Broughton would have shown it to me.'

'It's not in *the* Inverburgh Museum. That's quite reasonable. The silly old joker who handed it in had to go poking down the back streets and give it to the Wilton Collection. Nothing but a dust dump and you cannot get them to part with a thing.'

'Wish I'd seen it,' said Jinny. She liked the idea of worshipping a pony goddess, or, better still, a horse goddess like Shantih.

'Are you interested?' asked Freda.

'She is if it's horses,' said Mrs Manders.

'Well, why don't you ride over? Your mother has been telling us about your horse.'

'I'm not sure that I'll have time,' said Jinny doubtfully.

'Can't promise to produce another Epona while you're there, but we'd show you round the dig.'

'Could Sue come?' asked Jinny. 'To ride with me?'

'Why not? Bring sleeping bags, bunk down for the night and give us a hand the next day. Two ponies might bring us luck.'

Jinny hesitated.

'It would be very interesting,' said her mother.

Broadening my interests, thought Jinny.

'Not tomorrow, but the next day?' suggested Freda, making it definite where Jinny had hoped it would remain vague. 'Your father knows where the dig is. He'll show you where to come.'

'Well . . .' said Jinny doubtfully, thinking of course-building and jumping Shantih, and how there was so little of the summer holidays left, and then school and probably masses of homework. 'Well . . .'

But Freda was already out of the room, Ronald pattering behind her.

'So sorry to have troubled you,' Freda said, standing in the doorway as she said goodbye. 'One never knows, does one? Can't afford to ignore any clue.'

She was sitting in their Land Rover before she

24

remembered about Jinny.

'See you on Saturday,' she called, starting up the engine. 'And your friend.'

'It's not absolutely definite,' Jinny explained to her father as they went back into the house. 'She just mentioned that Sue and I could ride over and see the pace where they're excavating. It wasn't absolutely settled. We're going to build more jumps tomorrow and it really depends on how long that takes.'

'She invited you to stay the night,' said Mrs Manders. 'I think you should go.'

Mr Manders brought out his Ordnance Survey map and laid it on the table.

'That's where they are,' he said, 'staying in the old schoolhouse at Brachan. And that's where they're digging.' He traced with his finger.

'You could ride across the moors. You know your way to Loch Varrich. Ride along the side of the loch to there . . . and take that track that's marked right across the moors to Brachan.'

'Well . . .' said Jinny, knowing that it was something that she was always talking about doing, riding further that she had ever ridden before. She supposed there would be walls for Shantih to jump. 'I'll ask Sue tomorrow. Too late to go down to their tent tonight.'

Lying in bed before she went to sleep, Jinny was thinking about show jumps. Behind Mr MacKenzie's hay shed there was a discarded gate, and she was almost sure that he would never miss it. She would go over tomorrow morning and ask him if they could have it. They could paint it red and white and that would be almost as good as a real show jump.

Jinny remembered a chapter in one of her pony books that told you how to build a showjumping course. She got out of bed and went through to the other half of her room to look for the book.

When she found it, she leaned on the windowsill, staring out at the moors. They were patched with gulleys of black moon shadow and plains of blue silver moonlight. The mountains were dense velvet against the clear, cold sky. Jinny stared out, fascinated by this strange moonlit world, remembering how she had ridden Bramble over the moors at night.

What would it be like to take Shantih out on a night like this, to gallop and jump by moonlight? she thought, and Jinny was riding Shantih out into the night. She felt the Arab plunge forward into a gallop, felt her rise over the stone walls as she came to them, while Jinny balanced easily in the saddle.

Then suddenly, bringing her back from her dreaming, Jinny knew there was someone in the room with her, someone who had crept up close behind her. She sprang round, ready to be furious with Mike or whoever else it was. But the room was empty. No one was there. Only the yellow eyes of the painted Horse, luminous in the silver light, were staring directly at Jinny.

For a second she stood frozen to the spot, her fingers gripping into her arms, unable to move. Then she dashed across the room, dived into bed and curled under the bedclothes as if she was hiding from something, as if the painted Horse could come galloping out of the picture to find her.

Two

Shantih kicked her tail and fretted to be off as Jinny, poised to spring onto her back, tried to make her stand still.

'Whoa, Shantih, whoa. Stand now.' And Jinny leaped nimbly up onto the Arab. With a half rear, Shantih sprang forward, but Jinny was already sitting securely astride her.

'Oh no, you don't,' she warned her horse severely. 'Walk now.'

It was early morning. Jinny wasn't quite sure exactly what time because, as usual, both her watch and alarm clock had stopped. It felt about the right time for Mr MacKenzie to be finishing the milking, and that was a good time to ask him for anything you wanted. Later in the day he might be in the middle of doing something. He never looked busy and it wasn't easy to tell, when he was leaning on a half door smoking his pipe, whether he was in the middle of an important job or not.

Jinny let Shantih trot on along the lane to the farm. The morning air was crisp and sharp, a breath of autumn at the end of summer. Already the bracken was rust red on the hills, dried reeds were withering to flaxen, rowans were heavy with bunches of red berries, and here and there the trees were slashed with tints of autumn's orange and gold.

'Aye,' said Mr MacKenzie, pouring water from the churns he had been washing out, so that Jinny knew her timing had been right and he had just finished milking. 'You'll be up to no good raging around the countryside at this hour of the morning. What are you wanting?'

Mr MacKenzie lit his pipe and leaned against the byre door, willing to chat.

'I'm just out for a ride,' Jinny said, avoiding the direct approach.

'I can be seeing that for myself. It's the powerful amount of jumping you're putting in these days. We'll be seeing you on the telly the next thing we know. Only you'll need to be putting the jumps up a wee bit, I'm thinking. Ewan was watching you the other day and he was telling me your horses were shying with you on account of him not being able to see the jumps at all, they were that wee.'

The old farmer sucked on his pipe, spat and twinkled

out of the corner of his eye at Jinny.

'Remind me to give you fifty pence,' said Jinny. 'For the collection.'

'What collection would that be?'

'For Ewan's guide dog,' said Jinny.

There was an equal silence between them.

'You're not to be touching it,' said Mr MacKenzie, staring out beyond Jinny's head. 'It's a good enough gate and I'm not having it made into matchsticks by you two.'

'What gate?'

'Och, I saw you round the back of the hay shed with the red and white stripes in your eyes.'

'We wouldn't break it,' said Jinny, admitting the possibility of turning the gate into a show jump.

'That you will not, for you'll not be taking it. There's two hen coops – be having those if you want.'

'If,' said Jinny, who had already noticed the hen coops, 'we can get them to the field before they turn into dust.'

Mr MacKenzie had lost interest in the subject.

'Thanks anyway,' said Jinny, 'but I bet you never use that gate.'

'Aye,' said Mr MacKenzie, stuffing the bowl of his pipe with his blunt, nicotine-stained thumb.

Jinny jumped back onto Shantih and was about to ride away when Mr MacKenzie stopped her.

'What were they after?' he asked.

'Don't you know,' cried Jinny in amazement, for no matter what happened at Finmory Mr MacKenzie always seemed to know about it.

'I ken fine who they were – the fancy English with their spades digging up at Brachan. What I'm asking is what were they doing at Finmory.'

'They wanted to see the mural on my wall.'

'Now that is just what I was after thinking.'

'How could you know it was there?'

'Because it was myself was there when it was painted.'

'You?' said Jinny in amazement.

'Me,' said Mr MacKenzie. 'And I'll tell you something else that not one of them would be knowing. They should have been looking for the stone. Not that they'd be finding it today.'

'What *are* you talking about?' demanded Jinny.

'Seeing you're not everyone,' said Mr MacKenzie, 'I'll be telling you. When I was a boy, every spring the tinkers would be coming to Finmory to be painting up the Horse. It was carved on a stone that stood just by itself inside the gateway of Finmory House. They'd be touching it up with a spot of the red paint where it had washed away during the gales and be giving it the yellow eyes again. My old grandmother would take me to watch them. There was the gossip that my grandmother had the tinkers' blood in her, but I wouldn't be knowing the truth of that.'

'I've never seen a stone at our gates,' said Jinny. She had dismounted again so that she could listen properly to what Mr MacKenzie was telling her. 'The Red Horse is painted on the wall of my bedroom, not on a stone.'

'I'm telling you,' said Mr MacKenzie, 'if you'd be listening. It was one of the toffs blew the stone up so he could be making the fancy flower beds. Said it was a pagan thing.' He drew slowly on his pipe, then went on. 'When the tinkers had the word of the destruction, they were not for coming back in the spring as they had always done. Five years it was before we set eyes on them again. An old tink woman, and a lassie with hair as red as your own, came asking to speak with my grandmother. My father let them into my grandmother's bedroom. In a wee while she called my father in too. I was twelve at the time and fine I remember it all. When they came out, my father took the key of Finmory House, the toffs being away as usual for the winter, and they all went over to the house. I followed to see what they were up to and I went up with them to the servant's room – all dust and cobwebs it was. The old woman cleaned the wall, then she sat herself down in the dust and began her moaning and chanting while the lassie was painting the Horse on the wall, the same as had been on the stone.'

'But why on my wall?' demanded Jinny.

'They would be having their reasons, I don't doubt. But that's the truth of it.'

'So that was how it was painted,' said Jinny. 'I've always wanted to know.'

'Aye, that's how it was, though I dare say it will have been touched up since then. The tinks have their own ways of getting into an empty house. It's few have heard that story from me and why I should be telling you I couldn't say.'

'Because it's my bedroom now,' stated Jinny as she jumped back onto Shantih. 'And Sue and I might be riding over to Brachan to help them with their dig.'

'You'd be better doing no such thing. What the Old Ones were at was their own affair and nothing to do with the likes of yourself, but there's some people who can't leave anything alone, and I'm thinking you are one of them.'

'We're only going to watch,' said Jinny.

'Aye,' said Mr MacKenzie.

As Jinny rode home, the scarlet Post Office van drove up beside her and the postman handed up two letters to her. Neither was for Jinny. One was for her father and one was for Ken.

'You see,' Jinny said to Shantih, 'you are improving. You are much, much better. Only a month ago you'd have been all over the place if a van had come creeping up behind you like that.'

Jinny took Shantih's bridle off and left her in her loose box. After breakfast she would ride her over to Sue's tent.

As Jinny went into the house she looked at the letters. Ken's was an airmail from Holland, and her father's was from the Education Committee. Uneasily, Jinny wondered if it might be about her. *They shouldn't be able to get at you during the holidays*, she thought.

'Post,' called Jinny, going into the kitchen where her family were gathering for breakfast.

'For me?' asked Petra.

'Nope,' said Jinny, giving Ken his letter. 'And one for Dad from the Education Committee. That might be about you, complaining about the noise you make practising when the rest of the hostel is trying to sleep.'

Mr Manders came into the kitchen and took his letter from Jinny, looking at it quickly just in case it should be from the publisher who had his book.

'Whee!' exclaimed Ken. 'Listen to this. It's from Bob Schultz!' He looked round, his face lit up with surprise. 'From Bob Schultz!'

'Sorry,' said Petra, 'never heard of him.'

'You've heard of him, Tom?'

'No,' said Mr Manders.

'The potter. The only potter worth crossing the great water for. Saw some of his stuff in an exhibition in Stopton. Great stuff. Pots for the New Age. And the glazes he gets. Beautiful!'

'What's the letter about?' asked Petra.

'That's it. He's seen some of my pots, the ones Nell had at the Common Market exhibition. He liked them.

Wants to meet me in London next week. If I'm interested, he suggests I should go to Amsterdam for three or four months this winter to work with him in his pottery.'

'Oh great, Ken. That *is* good,' said Mrs Manders.

'It's what I need,' said Ken. 'To work with a master potter, and Bob Schultz is a master all right.'

'But you can't leave us!' exclaimed Jinny. 'We can't manage without you. *We* need you.'

'Don't be so selfish. Of course Ken must go,' said Mr Manders.

'Thanks,' said Ken. 'When I come back I might know what I'm about.'

Jinny turned her back on them, crossed over to the Aga. She couldn't bear the thought of Ken leaving. Not even for a few months. They needed him at Finmory. Jinny felt herself drowning in a black, unreasonable hopelessness.

'This toast isn't even pale brown,' she said crossly, picking up a slice of toast from the toast rack, but no one was listening to her.

'I've to phone Nell about the arrangements for London,' said Ken. 'She's coming too.'

Jinny scowled over her shoulder. 'Did Petra make it?' she demanded, still messing with the toast.

Mr Manders' letter was typed and official. When he had finished reading it, he held it out to Jinny.

'Really for you,' he said.

'Me?' said Jinny, reaching out for it but not wanting it.

Dear Mr Manders, she read. *We regret to inform you that due to unexpected delays in the building schedule of the new school at Inverburgh, it will not be ready to accept the September intake. Your daughter Jennifer Manders will therefore be attending Duninver Grammar School as a weekly boarder. A place has been reserved for her at the school hostel and further details will follow in due course. We apologise for any inconvenience which this unavoidable change may cause.*

For a moment Jinny didn't believe it possible. She stood staring at the letter and heard her father telling the others what was in it. They all looked at Jinny.

'Why, oh why,' exclaimed Mrs Manders, 'did this have to happen.'

'Tears and temper,' said Petra. 'Fuss, fuss, fuss, until she goes – and when you get there you'll love it. There's colour telly in the hostel and a super games room.'

'What about Shantih?' asked Mike. 'If Jinny goes to Duninver, who is going to look after Shantih?'

'You will have to go,' said Mr Manders. 'You must go to school.'

Numb and cold, Jinny stared back at them. She could not believe it. She felt tears brimming in her eyes, her nose beginning to run. She wanted to run away, to dash upstairs and hide in her bedroom.

Don't. Don't, Jinny told herself. *You mustn't run away*.

She squared her shoulders, pushed her long hair back behind her ears, and looked her father straight in the eye.

'I am not going to Duninver School,' she said. 'I am not going to the hostel there. I am not leaving Shantih.'

Jinny spent the rest of the day doing nothing but saying much the same thing over and over again. She was still saying it as she rode with Sue along the shores of Loch Varrich on their way to spend the night at Brachan.

'I'm not going and that's all there is about it,' Jinny stated fiercely.

'But you have to go to school,' said Sue. 'It's the law.'

'Then they can put me in prison,' said Jinny. 'I don't care. I'm not going.'

'You can ride Shantih at the weekends. It would be too dark to ride at night, anyway.'

'I'd be with her,' said Jinny. 'I could talk to her. But it's not just that. There is no one to look after her during the week. Daddy and Mummy won't even consider it. Petra's at the hostel, Mike hasn't time, and Ken is going off to this pottery place in Holland. So I *have* to stay. I cannot go to Duninver!'

Sue didn't answer.

'Do you know what they said? That I'd have to find somone to take her for the winter. They even suggested Miss Tuke.'

'If there's no one at home to look after her, you'll need to fix up something,' said Sue.

'I've told you,' snapped Jinny. 'I am not going. I've thought of several possibilities – enough money for a private tutor, a nervous breakdown . . . That could last till March – or even longer.'

'Oh, Jinny,' said Sue, laughing.

'Well, I must find some way. I must.'

Jinny gathered up Shantih's reins and sent her galloping over the moor, leaving Sue and Pippen far behind. She didn't stop until she had reached the head of the loch, where she halted Shantih and waited, watching Pippen's bumbling canter.

Sue will be mad, thought Jinny, *but at least she didn't see that I was nearly crying.*

Beyond Loch Varrich, the moorland rolled in waves to the far mountains. Stone walls, broken down by sheep and frost, ridged grey ribs through the heather. Except for the grazing sheep, there was no sign of any other life.

'You might have told me that you were going to gallop,' exclaimed Sue indignantly.

'Sorry,' said Jinny, meaning it.

'OK,' said Sue. 'But tell me next time. This place is like a desert, a heather desert.'

'I don't often ride as far as this,' said Jinny. 'So I don't really know the moor after Loch Varrich, but I should think this must be the track to Brachan.

There isn't another one.'

'Let's trot on,' said Sue. 'We don't want to be caught up here in the dark.'

The track they were following wasn't much more than a sheep track. It wound its way round rocky outcrops and barricades of gorse; it skirted silent, quicksilver pools that lay hidden in the heather like patches of sky.

After they had been trotting for a bit, Jinny halted Shantih and took the map out of her pocket. She spread it out over Shantih's withers and found the Brachan track on it, then tried to decide where they were. But she couldn't see any landmark, all around them there was nothing to be seen but rolling moorland.

'What are those little marks?' Sue asked, pointing at the map.

'Marsh,' said Jinny. 'The track seems to go right through it.'

'Well, that looks a reedy bit ahead now.'

'If it is the marsh, we're almost at Brachan.'

'About time too,' said Sue. 'You can feel it turning into evening.'

Putting the map back into her pocket, Jinny knew what Sue meant. The afternoon light had faded from the sky, leaving it steel grey and heavy. The moorland was closing into shadow.

'Only about another half hour,' said Jinny, trying to make her voice loud to fill the silence. 'Less, if we hurry.'

'Hope they remember we're coming,' said Sue. 'Perhaps they've forgotten about us.'

'Not the happiest thought,' said Jinny, letting Shantih jog on towards the marsh.

Soon the short, cropped turf changed into tussocks of reeds, and then into peat bog covered with a thin coating of half-dead, flaxen-coloured grasses. The horses' hooves sludged into the bog and came out with ominous squelching, sucking sounds.

'I wouldn't ride over this if the track wasn't marked on the map,' said Sue, from behind Jinny. 'I suppose it must be OK?'

Jinny made reassuring noises. She was standing up in her stirrups, balanced forward over Shantih's withers, taking her weight off her horse's quarters, and concentrating on following the track.

It was harder to follow now. The flat, peat bog had broken up into peat hags, each clod of peat surrounded by stagnant water. Shantih was picking her way across on top of the tussocks but twice her hind legs had slipped into the troughs between the peat hags. Her white stockings were black with mud and her belly splattered with gobbets of peat. She snorted unhappily through wide nostrils, wanting to swing round and gallop out of the bog.

'It's getting worse,' said Sue, her voice sounding strained and high-pitched. 'Are you sure it's OK to go on?'

Jinny didn't answer. Mr MacKenzie had once told her that it wasn't safe to trust maps that had been made several years ago; that one farmer changing the drainage on his land could affect the whole of the moor.

Quite suddenly there was no more track, only islands of peat bog surrounded by black, stagnant water.

'The track's stopped,' said Jinny.

'Isn't that it over there?' asked Sue, pointing ahead.

'Might be,' said Jinny. In the grey light she couldn't really see whether the track did go on or not. And even if it was the track there was a stretch of bog to be crossed before they reached it again.

Shantih pawed the ground, sending up sprays of water, then half reared in her anxiety to escape from the bog.

'What shall we do?' Sue demanded.

Jinny scowled. She was furious with herself for being so stupid as to ride into the middle of a peat bog. It was exactly the sort of thing her father and Mr MacKenzie were always warning her about.

'Even if we go back it won't be any better,' said Sue. 'We could easily get lost trying to find another way round.'

Jinny could hear the sucking, squelching voice of the bog all around her. She brought out the map and looked at it again.

'This must be right,' she said at last. 'Brachan must be in the next hollow.'

'Then we are almost there,' said Sue. 'We can't go back. It would be dark before we reached Finmory.'

'We're going on,' said Jinny, pushing the map back into her pocket. 'I'll go first. You wait here until I reach the track – that is, if it is the track.'

Jinny urged Shantih forward, forcing her to walk further into the bog when all the Arab's instincts told her it was not safe to go on.

'On you go,' muttered Jinny between gritted teeth. 'Walk on, get on with you.'

For the first few strides the ground was no marshier than it had been when they were following the track.

'Seems OK,' called Sue.

'Wait,' warned Jinny. 'Wait till I reach the track again.' Even as she spoke, Jinny felt Shantih's front legs sink into the bog.

Shantih gave a high whinny of fear as she struggled to free herself. She reared up out of the peat like a water horse, splattering water and slime. Jinny's hands were knotted in her mane, her heels drummed against her horse's side. She felt the power in Shantih's quarters as she surged forward and sank again, her chest straining, her neck crested and a high-pitched, desperate whinny of fear stretching her nostrils.

Suddenly, as they fought to escape from the quagmire, Jinny was sure she was being watched. Not by Sue and Pippen, but by something else. It was the same feeling as she had had that night when she had been alone in her room yet certain that someone else was there.

'Get on, get on,' she screamed at Shantih, driving her on with renewed urgency.

For one terrible moment Jinny thought that Shantih was going to be sucked down into the bog. Then Jinny felt Shantih gather herself together for a final effort, plunge forward and this time she didn't sink so deeply into the mire.

In another four or five strides they had reached the track again and Shantih was standing on firmer ground. Her plastered sides were heaving, her head low as she fought for breath, but they were safe. Jinny fell out of the saddle and leaned against Shantih. She couldn't have stood by herself.

'I'm coming,' yelled Sue, and Jinny watched helplessly as Pippen crossed the bog. Like Shantih, he plunged and fought his way through it, but his soup plate hooves stopped him from sinking into it as deeply as Shantih had done.

Jinny and Sue stared at each other, each seeing her own fear in the other's pale face.

'They'd have been excavating us,' said Sue.

'Peat bogs preserve skeletons,' said Jinny. 'They'd not have dug us up for thousands of years.'

They both began to laugh – high, hysterical laughter. It had been a near thing and they both knew it; the kind of thing you read about in the newspapers and can't imagine how anyone could have been so stupid.

'Come on,' said Jinny, leading Shantih away. 'Let's get on.'

Soon they had left the bog behind them. Glancing back over her shoulder at its black, glimmering water, and white, bleached reeds, Jinny swore to herself that she would never ride through it again. They would find a different way to ride home.

They remounted and rode on, until, from the top of a rise in the moors, they saw the excavation, and, a little further down the hillside, the few stone crofts that made up Brachan. Staring down at the piled rubble and earth of the dig, Jinny felt an uneasy coldness settle about her. They were disturbing things that belonged to the past, things that should be left alone.

Quickly, Jinny turned Shantih towards Brachan. She could see the square shape of what must be the schoolhouse. Smoke rose from its chimney, lights shone from its windows. There would be people and noise and warmth.

Hearing the sound of hooves, Freda and Ronald had come to the schoolhouse gate to welcome them and were suitably impressed by the state of their horses.

'What would your parents have said if you had sunk without trace? Still, as an archaeologist, one can't help feeling what a valuable find you would have been to the future.'

'Thank you,' said Jinny. 'Thank you very much.' She still felt chilled and uncomfortable. Not only because her feet were soaking and her jeans clinging muddily to her legs, but something else that she couldn't quite reach was troubling her.

Freda told them that a hot nosh-up would be ready when they were, and Ronald went with them to show them the field by the side of the school where the ponies were to spend the night.

When they went back to the schoolhouse, carrying tack and sleping bags, voices called to them to come in. Seven or eight people were sitting on the floor round a blazing log fire. Oil lamps were burning on the high windowsills. The bare schoolroom was softened with shadows. Freda introduced them, and a young man wearing a blue and white striped apron gave them mugs of soup and doorsteps of bread.

'Stew to follow,' he promised. 'Fifty-seven variety.'

Jinny and Sue found a place on the floor and drank their soup. At first the others asked them questions about their ride and their ponies, but gradually the talk returned to the excavation. Jinny leaned back against the wall and thought about Shantih. *I'm not going to Duninver*, she told herself. *I'm not leaving Shantih. They can't make me go.* But tonight Jinny was too tired to be able to think of how she was going to stop them.

Before they settled down for the night, everyone went out to the field to see Pippen and Shantih. Pippen was grazing, but Shantih was standing, alert and wary, looking over the moors towards the dig. At the approach of the strangers she flung herself away from them, tail and mane swirled and wild, her metal shoes glinting in the moonlight as she bucked. She turned back to face uphill again, her head outstretched as if searching for something on the moors that the humans couldn't see.

'She is Sleipner, the horse of Odin,' said a young man.

'Or the horse of the Wild Huntsman,' suggested someone else.

'She is the Horse worshipped by the Pony Folk,' said Jinny.

'If you mean Epona,' said Freda, 'she is usually shown with ponies, not Arabs.'

'Oh,' said Jinny, not knowing what she had meant, hardly knowing what she had said.

The schoolroom floor was very hard indeed. Jinny lay in her sleeping bag next to Sue and gazed at the dying fire. Already she was stiff and aching and she had only been lying there for about an hour. She was sure that she would never sleep; wished that she had never come.

Suddenly Jinny sat up. She was certain that she had heard Shantih neighing. She wondered if she should go out and take another look at her horse, but she didn't want to go out alone, not alone at night so close to the dig.

46

Jinny did not know much about the Celts, only that they had been a dark, magical people living in prehistoric Scotland. So long ago that Jinny's imagination could hardly reach them. And now, here at Brachan, their houses and graves were being disturbed.

Jinny listened intently but she didn't hear Shantih again. She lay down, still listening. Gradually her eyes began to close, then she woke with a start. The yellow eyes of the Red Horse were staring at her through the glowing embers of the fire.

Three

Jinny was back trapped in the peat bog. For as far as she could see, there was nothing but the black peaty water and the tussocks of dried reeds under a metal sky. At every step that Shantih took she sank deeper into the mire, until only her head and neck were visible. Then she would rear upright, her nostrils flared, her eyes huge with fear as she screamed her panic before she sank back into the bog.

On and on they went, sinking and rising, filled with blind terror, both knowing that the horror was about to begin.

Suddenly red light flashed over the metal sky, and above the rim of the marsh came the Red Horse. It stood braced for a moment, its head turning arrogantly as it surveyed the bleak landscape through its yellow eyes. It stretched out its neck and breathed in the essence of all the creatures struggling in its mire. It plunged to and fro as if uncertain where it would find the thing for which it was searching.

Jinny knew that it was looking for her. She tried to urge Shantih on, but the bog was closing over her. She could not turn her head to see if the Horse was coming any closer, only scream at the pitch of her voice.

'You were screaming all night,' Sue told her in the morning. 'I kept trying to wake you but you wouldn't. What were you dreaming about?'

'The Red Horse,' said Jinny, and she shuddered at the thought of her nightmare. 'It was searching for something.'

'Having bad dreams?' asked Freda, overhearing their conversation. 'You won't be the first to have bad dreams on a Celtic dig.'

'A woman I know,' said a young man, 'took home a Celtic stone head. She had to keep it in her house for two weeks before she could take it into the museum, and during those two weeks her husband, her son and herself all saw a small, dark man, dressed in skins, lurking in different places around the house.'

'You mean really saw him?' asked Sue.

'She said that when she saw him it reminded her of television – real but not real.'

'I believe that there are communities in Wales and parts of Scotland where they still follow the Celtic way of life, worshipping the Earth Mother in various forms,' said Freda.

'Well, I think it's all stupid,' said Jinny abruptly. 'Why do you have to go digging things up?'

'Perhaps they won't leave us alone,' mused Freda. 'We think we choose to excavate, but maybe the buried things choose us to set them free, to return them to where they should be.'

'Nonsense,' muttered Jinny. 'That's all rubbish talk. I don't believe a word of it.' And she walked away, not wanting to hear any more.'

After breakfast, Sue and Jinny were shown round the dig by one of the students. He showed them the circle of stones that marked the walls of the main house, the remains of the ring of posts that had supported the roof, and where they thought the fire pit had been. To Jinny it just looked like any other heap of mud and stones.

'I don't see how you can know,' she said stubbornly, as if by refusing to believe what the young man was telling them she could stop it being true. 'Haven't you found any skeletons?'

'No such luck. But we think the statuette of Epona was found round about here and we are hoping to find other evidence of horse worship.'

'You won't find it here,' stated Jinny. 'You're digging in the wrong place.'

'Is that a fact now?' said the young man, losing patience with Jinny. 'What would you know about it?'

Jinny couldn't tell him. She didn't know herself.

'Just feels wrong,' she muttered.

'A case of second sight?' asked the young man, and went on showing things to Sue, who was being bright and asking intelligent questions.

Sue and Jinny spent the rest of the morning carrying buckets of earth from one place to another. It was not the least like Jinny's idea of an excavation. It was all far too slow for her taste, with lots of exact measuring and marking going on. She hated the place. There was a cold eeriness about it that made the skin creep on the nape of her neck.

'We'll need to go immediately after lunch,' Jinny said to Sue.

'Wish we could stay another night,' said Sue.

'Well, we can't,' snapped Jinny. 'It's simply not possible.' Jinny had no intention of spending another night in the schoolhouse.

'All right. Keep your hair on. I only said I wished we could.'

'Well, I don't,' said Jinny, scowling. 'I wish we'd never come. I've more to do than waste my time here. Not like you. I've to teach Shantih to jump, and I've to sort out this mess about my school and I've my drawing. You've nothing to do compared to me.'

'How do you know I've nothing to do?' demanded Sue, startled by Jinny's sudden attack. 'You never did any jumping until I came.'

'I was just going to start,' said Jinny. 'It had

nothing to do with you.'

'It had a lot to do with my saddle. Before I lent you my saddle you could hardly stay on Shantih, never mind jump her!'

Jinny grabbed up her bucket of earth and marched away from Sue. She tipped the earth out onto the pile of rubble and stared round at the people working on the dig. She hated them all. They thought of nothing except measuring and labelling and locking things away in museums. And what did Sue know about riding a real horse? She only sat on Pippen. Jinny scowled to herself, drawing her brows down and setting the corners of her mouth. She didn't want to stay. She wanted to go home *now*.

'Is this the first dig you've seen?' a girl asked Jinny.

'Yes,' said Jinny.

'Fascinating, don't you think?'

'No,' said Jinny.

A cloud shadow blowing over the bracken looked, for a moment, like the shape of a great horse, mane tangled, hooves upraised.

'Look out,' yelled Jinny, jumping back, her arm shielding her face.

'Whatever's wrong?' asked the girl.

'I thought I saw . . .' Jinny's voice trailed into silence. The wind had blown the Horse away.

'Bet you it was a worm,' teased one of the students. Jinny opened her mouth to deny such a stupid suggestion, then thought it might be easier to let them think that. She smiled half-heartedly.

'A great big woolly one,' mocked the boy, as Jinny turned away.

'We can ride down the path from Brachan to Morston and then along the road to Ardtallon, through Glenbost, and then home,' Jinny told Sue, as she studied the map while they were eating their sandwich lunch. 'It's longer that way, so we'll need to go at once, the minute we've finished eating. I'm not trying to get through that bog again.'

'Not even with my saddle?' asked Sue.

'Sorry,' said Jinny. 'You're right. I couldn't jump without it.'

Sue grinned, 'And I can't jump with it because it gives Pippen a sore back.'

'I'm jolly glad it does,' said Jinny.

They said goodbye and thank you for having us to Freda, who said she was sorry they had to rush off and she'd be pleased to see them back any time.'

'Not me. Never!' said Jinny as she ran downhill to the schoolhouse. 'I'm not going back there. It's a foul place. I hate it. They should leave it alone.'

'Well, I thought it was very interesting,' said Sue, but Jinny didn't reply. She wanted to get back to Shantih as soon as she could, to be sitting astride her, trotting away from Brachan, away from the Celtic settlement, away from these people who didn't know what they were doing, disturbing hidden things.

They collected their sleeping bags and tack from the schoolhouse and walked over to the field. Pippen came bustling to the gate, but Shantih was still gazing out over the moors. Even when Jinny haltered her and led her over to the gate, she still went on staring out towards the dig, hardly paying any attention to Jinny.

'Ready?' asked Sue when they had saddled up and tied their sleeping bags to the fronts of their saddles.

Jinny had been waiting for Sue, watching the tiny figures working at the dig. She had become so intent, staring at the low stone huts, that she had hardly heard Sue's question.

'Are you ready?' repeated Sue. 'Oh, do wake up, you're dreaming again.' As Sue spoke, she led Pippen up to Shantih, meaning to open the gate and lead him through. 'Come on,' she said, reaching for the latch of the gate. 'I thought you were in such a desperate hurry to get away.' Shantih laid back her ears and glowered at Pippen.

'Get back,' Jinny shouted, her voice deep with authority. 'You have no right to bring a pony near the Horse.'

'What?' exclaimed Sue in astonishment. 'Whatever are you talking about now?'

'I don't know,' said Jinny, as surprised as Sue. 'I was staring at the huts on the moor, then I thought Shantih was going to kick and I said that.'

'What huts? There aren't any huts on the moor.'

'Up there,' said Jinny, but the cluster of low stone huts weren't there any longer. Now Jinny could only see the trenches and heaps of earth where they were excavating. 'But I saw them,' she said in bewilderment. 'They were there.'

'Well, they're not there now. And for goodness sake stop shouting at me!'

Jinny didn't try to argue. She led Shantih through the gate and mounted quickly. Her horse shied, dancing sideways, her tail kinked over her chestnut quarters as she waited impatiently for Sue to shut the gate.

The path from Brachan twisted over the moor. Jinny urged Shantih into a canter.

'I'm never going back there,' she swore. 'It's a foul place. I loathe it.'

Even when she reached the road, Jinny kept Shantih trotting on. The regular clip of the horses' hooves comforted her; the contact between the reins in her fingers and the bit in Shantih's mouth, the rhythmic strength of Shantih's stride and Sue riding beside her.

Jinny glanced back towards Brachan. She shuddered suddenly, goose over her grave. A cold fear clutched at her, for she knew that no matter how fast Shantih galloped, the Red Horse, moving with the speed of dream, must always be faster.

Jennifer Manders, Jinny told herself severely, *stop this nonsense. That dig has nothing to do with you.*

You have got to find some way of stopping them sending you to Duninver. That is what you've got to do.

That evening, Jinny's parents tried to talk to her about what was to happen to Shantih while Jinny was away at school.

'Have you thought about what you are going to do with Shantih?' her father asked.

'Thought of nothing else,' replied Jinny. 'But it is not going to happen because I am not going to Duninver.'

'Oh yes, you are,' said Petra smugly.

Mr Manders pushed his splayed fingers through his beard.

'Then where are you going to go?' he asked, trying to make it sound like a reasonable question, although he knew from the expression on his daughter's face that she had no intention of being reasonable.

'Perhaps I could stay on for another year at Glenbost?' Jinny suggested.

'And let Dolina go on to Duninver without you?' asked her mother, naming one of the other pupils from Glenbost who was the same age as Jinny.

'I don't care where Dolina goes. I don't care if she goes to university, as long as I can stay here with Shantih.'

'You do care,' said Mike.

'I could do the lessons they'd be doing at Duninver. I could manage myself as long as they sent the books to me. Or I'd buy the books myself and work here at home. Oh, Daddy, please.'

'Now you're being silly and you know it,' said Mr Manders sharply, cutting through Jinny's rising hysteria. 'You MUST go to Duninver.'

'I could have a tutor. The minister at Glenbost could be my tutor.'

Mr Manders ignored the suggestion.

'What we have to decide is what we are going to do with Shantih while you're away at school.'

'How can you say that?' cried Jinny. 'How can you say that? As if she was a car or a wardrobe or an old coat. It's like saying what will we do with Mike when we leave Stopton. Shantih is us. She lives here as much as I do. She's one of us. One of our family. I'm not going to *do* anything with her.'

'We're not suggesting you sell her. It's only for the winter. There is no one here who can look after her. She has to be stabled at night, you know that yourself. Do try to understand,' pleaded Jinny's mother.

'You're wasting your breath,' said Petra. 'She is going to make a fuss. You won't stop her.'

'I haven't time to look after her,' said Mr Manders. 'Even if I knew enough, I still wouldn't have time. If I don't work we don't eat. And your mother certainly couldn't cope.'

'You could if you tried,' Jinny said to her mother. 'I'd show you what to do.'

'I couldn't, dear. I don't know a thing about horses. I could not do it.'

'You don't need to ride her,' snapped Jinny. 'All you have to do is muck her out and lead her up and down to her field.'

'Jinny, I couldn't. You know there's far more to it than that.'

'Then Mike can look after her,' said Jinny, abandoning all hope of her mother becoming horsy.

'No,' said Mr Manders. 'He'll have his trekking pony to see to, his homework and riding to Glenbost. That is quite enough.'

'Oh please,' said Jinny, making her brother look at her.

'Not likely,' said Mike. 'She's all over the place when she has one of her crazy turns. And I wouldn't have time for anything else all winter.'

Jinny stared bitterly round her family. She thought of all the families she had read about in pony books who would have thought nothing of looking after a horse while their daughter was away at school.

No one had mentioned Ken. He would have looked after Shantih for Jinny. If he hadn't been going to this Dutch pottery place. For a moment, Jinny allowed herself to think that perhaps she could ask him not to go; plead with him to stay. He could go in the summer. He didn't need to go now. But she knew she mustn't even think of it.

'So the only thing we've been able to think of,' Mr Manders was saying, 'is to ask Miss Tuke to take her for the winter.'

'No! She'd want to ride her and try to school her. She'd turn her into a trekking pony. Shantih is my horse.'

'A little schooling would do her the world of good,' said Petra.

'And you like Miss Tuke,' said Mike, so that Jinny knew they had been discussing it while she had been at the dig.

'I'd drive you over to ride her every weekend,' promised her father. 'And if she was at Miss Tuke's you'd know that she was being well looked after. She's perfectly competent. Look how well she runs her trekking centre.'

'Shantih's my horse. I can't let anyone else ride her and school her. I can't. Miss Tuke is OK with her trekking ponies, but not with Shantih. She's all shouting and bossing. She only knows about hitting and kicking and shouting, "trek forward".'

Jinny's voice cracked on the edge of tears. She ran out of the room, through the hall and out of the house. Running as fast as she could, she raced through the garden and down to Shantih's field.

Shantih lifted her head from her grazing, ears pricked at Jinny's sudden approach, her dark eyes wide with surprise.

'They can't make me! They can't!' Jinny sobbed, flinging her arms round Shantih's neck and burying her face in her mane.

Miss Tuke was bossy and loud. She would sit on Shantih shouting, 'trek forward', as she did with the trekking ponies, and by the spring she would have turned Shantih into another of her trekkers.

It was dark when Ken came to find Jinny. He stood at the field gate and Kelly came across the field to Jinny, greeting her with low, wuffing barks, pushing at her legs with his wet nose, gazing at her through his grey, shaggy hair – his eyes glinting in the dark.

Jinny followed him back to Ken and they walked back in silence to the house.

Ask him if he'll stay. Ask him if he'll look after Shantih, said the voice in Jinny's head. But she couldn't She couldn't be so selfish.

She didn't go back into the front room where her family were still sitting, probably discussing how difficult she was being.

'Be easy,' said Ken. 'Listen to your breathing.'

But Jinny couldn't hear him. She went on alone, up the wide staircase, the bannister rail smooth under her hand, along the long corridor, and slowly, step by step, up the steep flight of stairs to her own room where the Red Horse and the nightmare waited for her.

Four

For the next two days, Jinny tried desperately to find some way of stopping them from sending her to Duninver School.

She went to see Miss Broughton, who had been her teacher at Glenbost School.

'So you see, I can't go to the hostel. I can't,' she finished, when she had explained the circumstances to Miss Broughton.

'It is maddening,' Miss Broughton had agreed. 'It all seemed to be working out so well for you – the new comprehensive opening up at just the right moment. I'm very sorry, but there is nothing I can do to change things.'

'Couldn't I come back here for another year,' pleaded Jinny.

'You certainly could not. A whole year stagnating

when you're ready to go on to a new school with a proper Art Department. Think of the other children you'll meet and the new friends you'll make. You wouldn't want to listen to Dolina talking about all the new things she's doing while you were still coming here.'

'Oh, I wouldn't mind. Truly I wouldn't mind,' declared Jinny.

'You think you wouldn't now, but you would by Christmas time. You would hate it. Anyway, the Education Committee wouldn't let you stay here.'

Jinny grunted in disgust. She supposed that she had better go and speak to the Education Committee herself.

She borrowed a matching scarf, handbag and gloves from Petra, put on her best skirt and jacket, and that afternoon she hitched a lift into Glenbost and caught the bus to Inverburgh.

'You want to see the Education Committee?' said the girl in the Education Offices, looking at Jinny suspiciously. 'What do you mean?'

'It's about the new school at Inverburgh not being ready in time.'

'Oh yes,' said the girl. 'We've had a lot of complaints about that.'

'Nothing like mine,' stated Jinny. 'I must see someone.'

'Perhaps Mr Scott would have a minute to speak

to you,' said the girl, lifting a phone on her desk.

'He'll see you now,' she said as she replaced the receiver. 'Come this way.'

She showed Jinny into a room furnished with filing cabinets and a large desk. Behind the desk sat a fat man.

'Sit down, little lady,' he said. 'And tell me what's troubling your little head.' So that Jinny knew at once that he wouldn't be any help. No one who called her a little lady could possibly be any use.

Mr Scott fumbled with the papers on his desk while Jinny tried to explain why she couldn't go to Duninver.

'Dear me, we do have problems,' he said when she had finished. 'I think the best thing you can do is to go straight home and ask your father to explain to you why your education is more important than bumping around on top of your gee-gee.'

Jinny stared at him in fascinated disgust.

'But one thing I can tell you, when the new term starts, you and all the other first-year pupils from your district will be attending Duninver School. There is no possibility of the school in Inverburgh opening in September. Gallop off with you now. I can't waste any more of my time over such rubbish.'

Jinny sat on the bus going back to Glenbost, seeing nothing, thinking nothing. A heavy certainty was squatting on her – the certainty that when the new term started she would be at Duninver School.

Back at Finmory she changed, caught Shantih and rode over to the field where their jumps were. The wooden boxes were still scattered from the night when Shantih had smashed her way through them; the night when Jinny had still been going to Inverburgh School; when the only thing that mattered was building a better showjumping course; before the archaeologists had come to Finmory.

The thought of the Brachan excavation made Jinny gather up Shantih's reins and send her cantering round the field, for last night she had dreamed the same nightmare. High and clear, Shantih soared over the jumps, while Jinny sat tight in the saddle, concentrating her whole mind on her horse.

That night the dream was waiting for Jinny again. It seemed that the second she closed her eyes she was back fighting her way through the marsh, while the Red Horse reared on the edge of the skyline, questing the air with trumpeting nostrils, its metal hooves sundering the earth, its yellow eyes searching, searching, while Jinny screamed.

'You've the banana face,' said Mr MacKenzie the next morning, when Jinny went over to the farm to see him. 'It's that jumping that's going for your liver. I was warning you for it.'

'I'm sick with worry,' said Jinny.

'Och now, I'm sorry to be hearing that. It'll be to do with the Inverburgh School, no doubt, and yourself having to be for Duninver with that fancy sister of yours.'

'Yes,' agreed Jinny. 'That's exactly what it is. I don't know what I'm going to do with Shantih.'

'I'm no surprised to be hearing that.'

'If they make me go to Duninver, please would you take her? Just Monday to Friday, really only Monday night to Friday morning. You'd only have to feed her and muck her out, put her in her field and bring her in again at night. I'd pay you for it. Please, please, Mr MacKenzie.'

'That I will not. I haven't the time to be carrying on with a useless brute like that one,' said Mr MacKenzie contemptuously. 'Was I not telling you from the beginning that she was not the horse for the likes of yourself to be having? That Pippen now, he's the horse for a lassie, not a wild beast like yon.'

'Thank you,' said Jinny. 'Let your "no" be "no". Enough.' And, carrying Finmory's milk, she trudged back home.

Petra was practising. Jinny hung around until she stopped and asked what Jinny wanted.

'Does anyone from Glenbost or Ardtallon travel to Duninver each day?' Jinny asked. 'Maybe someone whose father has a car and works there?'

'Why?' said Petra.

'I thought I could travel with them.'

'You're not allowed to. You must stay in the hostel,

it's a rule.' Petra returned to her practising.

'No,' said Mike, when Jinny asked him again if he would look after Shantih.

'Go on,' said Jinny. 'Please, please.'

'I can't,' said Mike. 'It's not as if she's going to be sold or shot or anything desperate. Then it would be different. Miss Tuke will look after her well. It's not long since you were wanting someone to school her for you.'

'*With* me not *for* me,' said Jinny. 'And now I'm teaching her to jump I can't have someone else riding her.'

'No,' said Mike.

Jinny went into the pottery and waited until Ken appeared. He sat down at the wheel and began to throw pots with quick, deft movements. Kelly lay, hearthrug at his feet, watching him.

'Do you really think you'll go to Holland?' Jinny asked, not looking at Ken.

'Anyone else but Bob Schultz and the answer would be "no",' said Ken. 'But I'll go for him. Heard him on the telly once. A plastic woman interviewing him and asking all the wrong questions. She said wasn't he afraid of running out of new ideas for his pottery and he stood up – he's a huge giant of a man, about six foot – and shouted, "Lady, my head is like a furnace, burning, blazing. My hands can't move fast enough to keep up with the ideas that come leaping through me".'

'Oh,' said Jinny politely. She didn't want to hear about Bob Schultz.

'So that's why I must go and work with him. The disciple approaches the master.'

'When are you going?'

'Going up to London next weekend with Nell. Probably Friday. She thinks he'll want me for the winter. Says he often takes on an apprentice during the winter when he's at his pottery in Amsterdam.'

Jinny picked up a lump of clay and began to mould it into different shapes. It wasn't a bit like Ken to be so enthusiastic about anything. Normally he said:

'"Sitting quietly, doing nothing,

Spring comes and the grass grows by itself".'

so she knew that he must really want to go. It wasn't just a notion.

Jinny began to make her clay into a pony shape. It wasn't up to Ken to say that he wouldn't stay and look after Shantih for her. It was up to her not to ask. She gave her pony a shaggy mane and thick tail. When she had finished she found a corner on the windowsill and left him there.

Then she ran out to Shantih, saddled her up and rode down to the bay. The Horton's tent was a bright square against the grass – but there was no sign of Sue or her family. On the sands, Jinny let Shantih gallop in wide circles, encouraging her to go faster, yelling into the sea silence and, when Shantih bucked, encouraging her to misbehave. Then Jinny cantered up to the field where the jumps were and rode Shantih at them.

'Go on! Go on!' cried Jinny as Shantih flew over them. She jumped her round again and again. When she was jumping Shantih Jinny forgot about the Red Horse, forgot about Duninver School and the thought of Miss Tuke taking Shantih away from her. There was nothing but the flying speed of her horse.

In the afternoon, Jinny went up to her room and shut her door with a bang so that her family would know she wasn't to be disturbed. Even at the very top of the house Jinny could still hear Petra's playing.

Thank goodness, Jinny thought, checking through her window to make sure that Shantih was safely in her field, then flinging herself flat on top of her bed, *her exam is on Saturday, then we'll get some peace.*

Mike was going to Stopton tomorrow to stay with a friend until the end of the holidays. Jinny thought he was mad.

'I don't really want to go,' Mike had said.

'Then don't,' said Jinny.

'But I promised I'd go back and stay with them. I didn't go last summer and I didn't go at Easter, and now his mother keeps on writing to Mum saying when am I coming and how much David is looking forward to seeing me again. I'd rather be here, but I suppose I'd better go.'

'I wouldn't.'

'Doesn't really matter,' Mike had said. 'It's only for a fortnight, and then we'll be back at school.'

A fortnight! thought Jinny, and in a sudden panic she jumped off her bed, brought her cash box down from the top of her wardrobe and emptied its contents out onto the top of her bed. She was saving up to buy a lungeing rein for Shantih. Nell Storr bought her pictures and sold them in her shop, but really Jinny wasn't very keen on selling her pictures to Nell. Once Nell had bought them, Jinny never saw them again.

Money, thought Jinny, counting out the eleven pounds that was in her cash box. *I'll need money whatever happens. If Dolina knows a farmer in Glenbost who would look after Shantih during the week I'd need to pay him, and I'd need more than eleven pounds.*

She would need to do more drawings for Nell. Jinny swept the money off the edge of the bed into the cash box. Quickly wrapped it up again in its Sellotape and put it back on the top of her wardrobe. She found her drawing pad, pastels and paints, and, sitting down on the floor, she began to draw.

Each drawing two pounds, Jinny thought. *Six drawings enough to keep Shantih for a week*. If *I can find someone in Glenbost who will keep her.*

A lump choked in Jinny's throat. She blew her nose hard.

Each picture two pounds, she told herself again. *Six pictures one week's keep. Twenty-four pictures, one month.*

Jinny forced herself to go on painting as fast as she could. Nell had said that her customers liked the drawings of Shantih best, so Jinny painted Shantih – Shantih's head, Shantih grazing, Shantih galloping and Shantih jumping. If a bit of her drawing didn't look quite right, Jinny smudged it over. She drew grass round Shantih's hooves so that she didn't have to waste time with difficult fetlocks and pasterns; she painted swirling manes and tails to cover up necks that were too long or hocks that bent in an odd way.

All the drawings were hopeless and Jinny knew it. Even the ones that looked all right weren't of Shantih. They could have been any chestnut Arab. Normally, Jinny would have torn them all up and gone for a ride.

They're very good, she told herself, arranging them in rows of weeks and months. *As good as lots of the pictures you see in shops. Better. Nell will never know the difference. She doesn't know anything about horses.*

Jinny shuffled the pictures into a pile, not wanting to have to look at them again for they were all so bad.

She wandered through to the other half of her room, feeling gritty and cross with herself. Absorbed in her painting, she had forgotten about the Red Horse.

The glowing yellow eyes were waiting, glaring out

at her. Jinny stood still, staring back at the Horse. It was a rough, crude drawing. The Horse's legs were too long. Its head was out of proportion to the rest of its body. But it was alive. It crashed through the branches straight at Jinny. The yellow circles of its eyes commanded her.

Jinny brought paper and pastels, and, kneeling on the floor in front of the Horse, she began to draw. Her hand moved, knowing by itself what to do, and on the paper in front of her Jinny saw her dream take shape – the peat hags sprouting their dead crowns of withered reeds, the black water and the metal sky, tight and suffocating as a killing bottle being pressed down on top of her. Then her fingers found the orange and red and yellow pastels – the fire colours – and the grey sky glowed with the coming of the Horse.

On the next sheet, Jinny's hand drew herself and Shantih struggling to escape from the black peat bog, the sky above them burning, molten.

On the third sheet of paper the Red Horse reared over the horizon, red-gold, burning, seeking. Its head was flung upwards, forelock blown back in the burning winds, yellow eyes flaming, as it searched for the thing it had come to find.

Kneeling on the floor, Jinny waited, unable to move. The pictures she had drawn held her captive.

Voices came from below. A woman's voice, loud and brisk, and then her father's voice shouting her name.

Unmoving, Jinny swam towards the sound. She heard her father's footsteps coming along the landing and stopping at the foot of her stairs.

'Jinny! Jinny!' he called. 'Come down. Miss Tuke is here to see you.'

Jinny struggled to her feet. For seconds, the power of the Red Horse still held her – and then she broke free. She scrabbled the drawings of her dream together and hid them under the pile of drawings she was going to take to Nell Storr's shop.

'Jinny, are you up there?'

'Yes, I'm here,' Jinny yelled back, and she went pounding downstairs to her father.

'What's Miss Tuke doing here?' she demanded. 'Did you phone her? Did you?'

'No,' said Mr Manders. 'I did not. You know I wouldn't have done that without asking you first.'

'Well, why is she here?'

'To find out what trekking ponies we need for the winter. But now she is here we may as well take the opportunity and ask her about Shantih?'

'No,' said Jinny.

'Only ask. There's no point in going on arguing about whether or not Shantih is to go to Miss Tuke's when Miss Tuke may not even be willing to take her.'

Jinny followed her father down to the kitchen where Miss Tuke was sitting at their huge oak table having a cup of tea with Mrs Manders.

'Didn't you hear us calling you?' asked Mrs Manders. Jinny shook her head.

'What were you doing?'

'Drawings,' said Jinny. 'To sell to Nell Storr.' She didn't mention the Red Horse, how it had come out of the painting, making her draw her dreams, how it was still there on the edge of her mind, always there, waiting.

'I came to see you about ponies,' said Miss Tuke. 'Your mum tells me you won't be needing one. You're off to Duninver to the school hostel. Quite a change from battling against the gales on Bramble. I hear it's utter luxury.'

'I don't want to go,' said Jinny.

'Who is going to look after that mad Arab while you are away?'

'It's rather a problem,' said Mr Manders. 'In fact, we were going to get in touch with you and see if you might consider taking her for the winter?'

'Were you?' said Miss Tuke. 'Now that's a thought. I always do stable one or two of my favourite Highlands so I have something to ride when the trekking is over. I was going to hang onto Shona this year, but I've had rather a tempting offer from a family who trekked with me for a fortnight and fell for her in a big way. Might be rather fun to have something like Shantih. Never had much time for Arabs. Fidgety beasts. But for a few months . . .'

Jinny didn't look up. She picked at the corner of the table, scowling.

'Of course I'd pay something towards her keep. We can't manage to look after her here when Jinny is away, so we would be most grateful.'

'What has Jinny to say about it?' asked Miss Tuke.

'It's not going to happen. I'm not going to Duninver.'

Jinny felt her parents and Miss Tuke smiling at each other, being adult and sensible.

'Wouldn't do the mare any harm to spend a month or two with a stronger rider,' said Miss Tuke. 'From what I've seen and heard of her, she has a will of her own. Gets the better of you more than sometimes.'

'Not now,' stated Jinny. 'That's past. I'm teaching her to jump now.'

'Would you consider it?' Mr Manders asked.

'Could I have a ride on her? I've an hour to spare. My trekkers are morning and evening today.'

'Certainly,' said Mr Manders. 'OK, Jinny?'

And somehow they were all out of the house and walking down the path to Shantih's field. Shantih looked up from her grazing, nostrils flurrying a welcome, and came towards them with her exact, precise step. Jinny slipped the halter over her ears and led her back towards the stables.

'Hey. Hi there,' called voices, and across the fields came Sue, trotting on Pippin, and Mrs Horton running behind her.

'Deary me,' exclaimed Mrs Horton, out of breath as she caught up with them. 'Need to do something about this flab.'

'Oh, Mummy!' said Sue.

'All right for you young things. Wait till you're my age. It creeps up on you.'

Mrs Manders said she knew how it felt and that she too was being crept up on.

'A few weeks' trekking and you'd soon be fit again,' said Miss Tuke.

'That's what we want to see you about,' Mrs Horton said. 'We saw you drive past in your van. Pine Trekking Centre?'

'That's me,' said Miss Tuke.

'Could we trek for a day this week?'

'Certainly. How would Thursday suit?'

'Very well. My husband and I haven't done any riding before, but with Sue having Pippen we're into horses, as they say, and we thought that before we go home this year we would have a shot at riding them.'

'That's the spirit,' encouraged Miss Tuke. 'Two on Thursday. Full-day trek.'

'Three,' corrected Mrs Horton. 'Sue is coming too. And Jinny?'

'It's too expensive,' said Jinny. 'I can't afford it.'

'Jinny can ride Bramble,' said Miss Tuke. 'We'll call it a reunion. No charge.'

'I don't know if I'll have time . . .' Jinny said, but no

one was listening to her. They all took it for granted that she would go. Jinny supposed that it would be nice to see Bramble again.

'Thursday, then,' said Mrs Horton. 'That's a definite booking. Hail or snow, we will be there.'

Mrs Manders, Mr Manders and Mrs Horton went back to Finmory while Jinny saddled up Shantih. Miss Tuke gathered up her reins and mounted. Her toe dug into Shantih, making the Arab spring away from her.

'Stand, you twister,' bawled Miss Tuke as she struggled into the saddle. Her hands clutched at the reins, making Shantih fling her head into the air and Jinny wince.

'Tell you one thing,' Miss Tuke shouted to them. 'If I take her she'll stand to be mounted before I've finished with her. Never had a Highland yet that didn't learn that lesson. You couldn't have trekkers behaving like this.'

Jinny wanted to shout back that it had been Miss Tuke's toe digging into her side that had made Shantih spring away, but, before she had time to reply, Miss Tuke was riding Shantih round the field.

Sue, Pippen and Jinny watched from the field gate, Pippen resting his blubber chin on the top bar, half closing his eyes.

When Miss Tuke trotted, she banged up and down on Shantih's back, her hands clamped heavily on the reins, her solid legs tight against Shantih's sides. There was no sweetness in her riding, no feeling for her horse. Miss Tuke might as well have been driving a tractor.

'All right to canter?' bawled Miss Tuke.

'Yes,' said Jinny, because there was nothing else she could say.

Miss Tuke kicked Shantih into a canter, but instantly her hands pulled on Shantih's reins to slow her down again. Shantih battered round the field at a ragged, unbalanced trot.

'Canter, you idiot,' yelled Miss Tuke, scarlet in the face as she held Shantih's mouth in a stranglehold and kicked her Wellington boots into Shantih's sides.

'She's not much of a rider,' whispered Sue. 'But she wouldn't be scared of Shantih.'

Jinny had turned away. She couldn't bear to watch any longer.

'She'd ruin her,' said Jinny bitterly.

'Of course, we'll need to discuss details,' said Miss Tuke when she dismounted, 'but if you do want me to take her I'd be quite willing to consider it. We'd have some good rides wouldn't we, old girl? Soon get some sense into your noddle.' Miss Tuke clapped Shantih's neck with her broad, capable hand. 'Must be off. See you both on Thursday.'

'Come for a ride,' suggested Sue, when Miss Tuke had driven away.

'Where to?'

'Over the moors?'

Jinny glanced quickly up at the moors. They stretched, flaxen, bronze and purple, to the far mountains. The afterglow had faded from the sky. Light came from the rust-gold bracken.

'Let's jump,' said Jinny. 'In the field.'

'Oh no. Come for a ride.'

'I want to jump.'

'If you jump Shantih much more over those same jumps you'll sicken her for life.'

'Won't.'

'Well, I'm going for a ride.' Sue turned Pippen and began to ride towards the moors.

For a moment Jinny hesitated, wanting Sue's company, wanting to be chatting and laughing together, the way it had been at the beginning of the holidays. Almost, she called to Sue to wait, almost, she sent Shantih trotting after them. But she didn't. She watched Pippen's skewbald quarters and Sue's straight, square-set back climb towards the moors, then she rode Shantih to the field where the jumps were.

Seeing the jumps, Shantih began to prance with excitement, tossing her head and clinking her bit. Jinny leaned her weight forward in the saddle, her knees tight, her feet braced against the stirrups, and Shantih surged forward. She soared over the jumps, her forelegs tucked in, close to her body, forelock blown back, her face hollowed by her speed, her eyes alight.

'Again,' whispered Jinny.

She didn't want Shantih to stop. Wanted her to go on jumping, on and on. It was only when she was jumping Shantih, absorbed in the thrill of her pounding hooves and soaring leaps that Jinny felt safe, that she was able to forget the Red Horse. All the rest of the time it was there, haunting the edges of her mind, waiting for her to fall asleep so that it could come, brazen and terrible, charging into her dreams.

Five

Jinny cantered Shantih back to her field. She had been up since five o'clock, jumping in the field in the chill, early morning and now she was sure she was late. This morning, Ken and her father were taking Mike to Inverburgh to catch the Stopton train. Then they were taking a load of pottery to Nell Storr's craft shop. Jinny had to go with them. She had to get the money from Nell for her paintings and find out how many more Nell would be willing to buy.

Jinny took off Shantih's tack in her field. Not even waiting to see Shantih roll, she shut the gate and ran up to the tack room. She flung down the bridle and placed Sue's saddle carefully on a rack.

'Why someone doesn't give me a watch that works, I don't know,' Jinny cursed as she ran up to the house. She felt tight and cross, as if she wasn't properly there.

Last night her dreams had been worse. The Red Horse closer than before. Huddled under her bedclothes, Jinny had lain petrified, afraid of the painting on her wall, afraid of falling back into her dream.

'I'm coming with you,' Jinny yelled to her family who were gathered at the front door, saying goodbye to Mike.

'Where have you been?' asked her mother.

'Jumping,' Jinny called back, racing upstairs three at a time.

'We're going NOW,' shouted her father. 'We haven't time to wait for you.'

'I'm ready,' yelled Jinny.

In her room she snatched up the pile of drawings and turned to race back downstairs.

Mr Manders was at the wheel, Ken and Mike getting into the car.

'Wait! Wait!' shouted Jinny, flinging herself through the hall and out of the door.

'You haven't had any breakfast,' said her mother despairingly.

'And look at your hair. You haven't even brushed it,' said Petra.

Jinny ignored them. She jumped into the back of the car with Mike and collapsed, gasping for breath.

'Didn't know you wanted to come,' said Mr Manders, driving down the road. 'Another minute and we'd have been away without you.'

'I thought you weren't even going to say goodbye,' added Mike.

''Course I was,' said Jinny. 'I'll miss you.'

'You will,' agreed Mike. 'You'll need to go for the milk every day.'

'You'll need to do a fortnight when you come back,' said Jinny.

'I'll need to do a whole term,' said Mike. 'You'll be at Duninver.'

Jinny felt her blood run suddenly cold. It wasn't true. It couldn't be true – that Mike was going to Stopton and when he came back she was to go to Duninver, Shantih to Miss Tuke's.

Standing on the station platform waving goodbye to Mike, Jinny saw his departure as the first in a series of events. Now Mike had gone, all the other things must happen, like a row of dominoes all having to fall once the first one had been knocked over.

'Enjoy yourself,' called Mr Manders, waving. 'Send us postcards.'

Mike's head and waving arm vanished round the curve of the track. He had gone. Jinny walked, cold and miserable, back to the car. She curled into the corner of the back seat, wishing desperately that Mike hadn't had to go away just now. With the Horse so close she needed all her family to be with her, to make Finmory a safe place where she could hide.

'Joy to see you,' Nell Storr greeted them, opening

the doors of her shop so that Ken and Mr Manders could carry in their crates of pottery. 'Pile them up. Your shelves are nearly empty again.'

Jinny helped to stack the pottery on the shelves, then she followed Ken and her father into Nell's office at the back of the shop. Normally, she would have been prowling around, looking at the carvings and weavings, the embroideries and silverware which filled the shop, but today she only wanted to show her pictures to Nell, to find out how much she would pay for them.

'Four orders for mugs and coffee pots. A woman at that phone number wants to know if you'd be interested in making a chess set for her with pottery pieces. And how do you feel about some Christmas things – hanging plates, Christmas bowls, candle holders?'

Nell Storr was wearing a black and purple velvet dress. When she moved, it seemed to flow around her like theatre curtains, Jinny thought. Her Afro hair was dyed orange, her lips painted to match her hair, and her long fingers knuckled with rings.

'Quite a turn up for the book, Bob Schultz liking your stuff,' Nell said to Ken. 'Seems he walked into the exhibition, more or less went straight over to the stall where my lot were on show, picked out your pots, asked where they'd come from and said he'd found his apprentice for this winter. Lucky you. Wouldn't mind spending a few months in his pottery myself.' Nell raised her eyebrows in mock despair at the confusion of papers and samples in her crowded office. 'I'm going up to London on Friday for the weekend,' she said. 'You can drive up with me. Bob Schultz will be there, and we've to get in touch with him when we arrive.'

'Great,' said Ken.

'He wants to meet you before anything definite is decided. You don't need to worry, though – from what I've seen of him he's as silent as yourself. You'll get along.'

Ken's slow smile spread over his face, lighting his eyes, lifting the corners of his lips.

'And he's a vegetarian.'

'I guessed,' said Ken, laughing.

But Jinny could only think that next weekend was Petra's piano exam; that Ken, her mother and Petra would all be away at the same time; that already Mike had gone.

'I've brought you some more drawings,' Jinny said, when Nell had finished talking to Ken.

'Good,' said Nell. 'You have been busy,' she added, seeing Jinny's pile of paintings. 'I am honoured to have all these. Let's see them.' Nell cleared a space on her desk.

Jinny spread out her paintings and drawings of Shantih. She hadn't looked at them since she had finished them, and now, with Nell, her father and Ken all looking at them, Jinny realised how very bad they were. She laid them out quickly, trying to cover up the worst. The last three drawings were of her nightmare. Jinny hadn't meant to bring them with her. She had forgotten that she had hidden them under the others when Miss Tuke had arrived. She hid them behind her back and waited in the uncomfortable silence while Nell flicked through the paintings.

'You did these?' Nell asked at last.

'All of Shantih,' said Jinny, trying to sound confident and enthusiastic. 'You said they liked Shantih best, that you wanted more of her.'

Still Nell didn't speak. She laid the worst ones back on the desk, then she looked straight at Jinny, lifting her eyebrows questioningly.

'They won't do,' she said. 'What went wrong?'

Jinny felt herself going red.

'I thought you wanted more of my drawings,' she mumbled.

'Not this trash,' said Nell. 'I wouldn't sell them, even if I could.'

'They're OK,' said Jinny. 'You have to buy them so that I'll have enough money to pay for Shantih.'

'But I'm going to pay Miss Tuke,' said Mr Manders.

'Oh not Miss Tuke!' snapped Jinny. 'Shantih's not going to her. I'm going to find someone in Glenbost who'll take her.'

'They've no magic,' said Nell, shuffling the rejected pictures together. 'No life. To create, you have to tear out your own heart and not expect to get it back. You haven't torn out a single hair for these. Let's see the ones you're hiding behind your back.'

Reluctantly, Jinny produced the three drawings of her nightmare.

'Ah ha! Come on now,' said Nell. 'I'll buy these from you. In fact, I'll buy the one of the horse for myself. Fifteen pounds?'

'Nightmares?' asked her father, looking searchingly at Jinny. 'We thought we heard you screaming in your sleep. Have you dreamed about this often?'

'All the time,' said Jinny, and she bit into her lower lip to stop it shaking.

'Sue told me you were both nearly bogged down on the way to the dig. Is that what's giving you the nightmares?'

'Am I glad that horse chose you and not me. Can I have him?' asked Nell.

Jinny shook her head. Fifteen pounds would be no use to her. Who would look after Shantih for fifteen pounds? And she would never have enough time to paint real pictures of Shantih. Before she could paint the kind of pictures Nell wanted, Jinny had to see what she was going to paint clearly in her mind's eye; know it before she could paint it.

Ken was looking at the nightmare drawings, holding them carefully in his long, bony hands.

'The Horse in the mural?' he asked.

Jinny nodded.

'What mural?' asked Nell, and Mr Manders explained, adding that she must come out and see it some time.

'You'll have seen the little statue of Epona?' Nell asked Jinny.

'Freda, the archaeologist at the dig at Brachan, mentioned her. Said the Celts used to worship her,' said Mr Manders.

Hearing the word Epona spoken out loud sent shivers up and down Jinny's spine. You shouldn't speak of a goddess like that, not out loud where anyone could hear you. She wanted to warn Nell but couldn't find the words.

'You haven't seen her? Oh, but you must visit the Wilton Collection. I'll take you now. Some rather nice pottery – and Jinny must see Epona.'

'Yes,' said Jinny. 'I must. Let's go now.'

Suddenly it didn't matter that Nell hadn't taken her drawings. To see Epona mattered more than anything else. Yet it wasn't like wanting to see something new, more like going back to Stopton to see one of her special places again, to go at once in case it should have changed.

'You really won't sell me the horse?' Nell asked. 'I'll make it twenty.'

'No,' said Jinny. She needed her drawings. Somehow, to have drawn her nightmare gave it less power.

'Sorry I can't take the others.'

'Doesn't matter.' Jinny tore her other pictures into pieces and dumped them into Nell's wastepaper basket. 'I knew they were no good.'

'Going out for an hour,' Nell called to her assistant, and led the way out of the shop.

'Only five minutes,' she told them. 'We don't need to take the car.'

'You'll love the Wilton Collection,' she said as they walked along. 'Belongs to an old boy, ninety odd he must be now. All things collected by himself and his two brothers. Some very valuable stuff. The big museums are always on at him to let them take over his collection. Saying it is inadequately protected and that sort of guff. But no one ever seems to steal it. Just the opposite. You're always reading in the local paper that someone or other has died and left things to the Wilton.'

People in the street turned to look at them – Nell in her flowing gown, Mr Manders, balding with his red beard, and Ken, bleach-blond as if he had been washed by the tides.

Next time I shall be riding Shantih. The thought came into Jinny's head as if a voice had spoken it, a mad thought, for how could she ever ride through the Inverburgh streets, which were crowded with double-decker buses, cars, vans and lorries?

Nell turned down a side street where the high

tenement buildings had an indrawn grace. She stopped by a plaque that announced The Wilton Collection – Open To The Public Monday to Saturday, 9 a.m. to 7 p.m. Admission Free.

Nell pushed open the outside door and they all climbed up a wide staircase to a long corridor. On either side of the corridor were glass exhibition cases, and on the walls were shelves of vases and pots. There was no sound. The thick walls absorbed all the noise of the Inverburgh traffic. For a moment they stood in silence, surrounded by the watching objects.

'George must be having his cuppa,' said Nell. 'He usually is. I'll introduce you later. Quite a character. Been caretaker here for fifty years.'

She walked on. 'Now for Epona.'

They followed Nell into one of the three rooms leading off the main corridor. The windows were stained glass, colouring the dusty light. The display cases around the room were old, made of dark wood and thick glass. Nell led the way to a small case in the corner.

'Here she is.'

Jinny had crossed the room with Nell, her throat and mouth suddenly dry and her heart lumping and thumping. Her mind felt like a kite pulling away from her body so that she seemed to be looking down on the room. It was a giddy, slipping feeling, making her hold onto the display case with both hands.

The statue of Epona was about six inches high. A woman with a round head, and wearing a long, sweeping dress, was seated sideways on a heavy, native pony. In one hand she held the reins and in the other a round fruit. There was no detail in the statue, only the simple shapes. The woman, the thickset pony and the fruit in her open hand.

Jinny stood without moving, hardly breathing. Vaguely she heard the others saying that they were going to look at some pottery as they left her alone.

The woman, the pony and the fruit.

Jinny felt the edge of the case move under her grasp. The wood round the lock had decayed into dry tinder. Jinny forced the lid of the case open. The lock lifted out of the rotten wood. She saw her hand reach into the case and lift out the pony goddess. Jinny held it in her open hand. From a corner of the ceiling her mind watched and recorded. The little statue seemed to pulsate with a beat of stored energy. It seemed to grow and swell, dwarfing Jinny. Words long forgotten, long buried, struggled to be heard again.

Voices came from one of the other rooms, footsteps crossed the corridor. The others were coming back. For endless seconds, Jinny couldn't move her arm, couldn't make it put Epona back into the case. It seemed certain that they must find her holding it. At the last possible moment Jinny broke the spell, forced herself to return the statue to its case and close the lid.

The others came into the room. Loud and violent they came straight towards her. Jinny turned to face them. Words came out of her mouth in a voice that was her own and not her own.

'Not one,' she said, 'but one.'

'Surely you must know what you meant,' persisted Mr Manders as they drove home. 'When you say something you must know why you've said it.'

'But I don't,' said Jinny miserably. 'I just say things. I don't know I'm going to say them.'

'"The kraken waketh",' quoted Ken, which didn't seem to make much sense either.

'There's a letter for you,' Mrs Manders said to her husband when they reached Finmory again, but Mr Manders had seen it the second he had walked into the room – a long, white, foolscap envelope lying on the sideboard. He picked it up quickly. It had a typed address, a London postmark. It might just be from the publishers who had his manuscript. He tore it open and pulled out the letter.

'Someone wanting info on one of my Stopton boys,' he said, putting the letter down and going to make himself a cup of tea.

'Next time,' said Mrs Manders.

'But they've had it for ages,' said Jinny. 'Weeks and weeks. I'd phone them to find out what's happening to it. Maybe they've lost it.'

'I'll write in another fortnight,' said Mr Manders.

'I have the date ringed on my calendar when I give in and write to them.'

'At least you would know,' said Mrs Manders.

'Better to travel hopefully,' said Mr Manders.

Jinny heard Sue riding up to the back door, and went out to see her.

'Hi! Smashing day,' said Sue. 'What are we going to do?'

'Nothing special,' said Jinny warily. What she really wanted to do was to stay at home, safe and secure in Finmory with her family round about her.

'Come for a ride,' begged Sue.

Jinny shook her head. She didn't want to go out onto the moors. Even the moors round Finmory that she knew well weren't safe when the Red Horse was looking for her.

'Oh, please. It's so much better when you come. I can have a gallop when you're there. When I'm alone I'm always sure I'm going to break Pippen's legs.'

'Let's jump,' said Jinny.

'Mr MacKenzie says you've been jumping already this morning.'

'Trust him to see me,' said Jinny in disgust.

'You can't jump again. Not so soon. You really will sicken her. Come for a ride. I only have nine more days left.'

Jinny was shocked. She couldn't imagine life at Finmory without Sue. The summer holidays had been going on forever. Sue and Pippen had always been there.

'So please, please, please, do come for a ride.'

'Oh OK then. After lunch.'

'I feel,' Jinny announced to her family at lunch, 'as if fate is against me. As if all the worst things are zooming straight at me.'

'Do you want more pie?' asked her mother, and even Ken was talking to her father about shops in London where they could buy things they needed for the pottery.

'Where do you want to go?' Jinny asked Sue when they had both mounted.

'To the standing stones,' said Sue, and began to ride Pippen along the path to the moors.

Jinny opened her mouth to shout after her, to tell her that she wasn't going near the stones, but she couldn't make a sound. She tried again as Shantih trotted after Pippen, but her voice croaked in her throat.

Waves of moorland flowed out behind them as they rode towards the stones. The mountains were metal ridged, sharply defined against the sky. Sue was chatting about cavalletti but Jinny wasn't listening.

The jagged teeth of the standing stones came into sight over a rise in the moorland. Jinny felt as if they were waiting for her, drawing her towards them. Shantih was playing up, shying and fretting, refusing to walk. Jinny sat down hard in the saddle, forcing her to walk on.

'What's got into her today?' said Sue, watching Shantih's antics from the safety of Pippin's broad back, his steady plod.

A heron flew up from one of the pools in the heather. Shantih reared straight up, stood poised on her hind legs. Jinny clutched at handfuls of mane. For a moment she was certain that Shantih must overbalance and fall. She heard Sue scream, and the harsh *craak* of the heron, then Shantih had touched down again, half reared, and thrown herself forward into a flat-out gallop.

By the time Jinny had managed to stop her, they were almost at the standing stones. No longer were they teeth in the distance, but towering blocks of stone, standing in a broken ring, crowning this height of the moor. Shantih's mouth was white with froth, her chest foam-flecked, and her sides darkened with sweat. She stood shaking, her head down, as Pippen came trundling across the heather to reach them.

Suddenly Shantih threw up her head, ears alert, eyes wide. She whinnied, but she wasn't calling to Pippen, she was calling to something behind the stones.

The low sun shone directly between two of the upright stones, blinding Jinny. Its light glistened on Shantih's eyeballs as she stood, tense and tight, her neck arched and hard. Sitting on her, Jinny knew she had lost all control over her horse. Shantih had forgotten that there was anyone riding her.

Shantih whinnied again, a clarion blast of noise.

The sound rolled over the moors. The echoes died, and in the silence that followed Jinny heard the thunder of hooves coming from behind the standing stones. She felt the ground shudder with their impact, felt the moment of indrawn breath before the terror burst upon her.

And in that moment Jinny had pulled Shantih's head round, sawing at the bit, kicking her heels in her horse's sides, cracking the slack of the reins against her neck and screaming at the pitch of her voice. Anything, anything to escape from the hooves that were thundering down on her from behind the black of the standing stones.

Shantih saw the reins flap against her neck. Almost-forgotten memories of the circus, and the ringmaster's whip, stirred in her memory. She flung herself away from the whip, away from the reins. The movement was enough to allow Jinny to make contact with her horse again. She urged her into a furious gallop away from the stones.

When Sue eventually caught up with them, Jinny had dismounted and was leaning over Shantih's withers, her face hidden.

'What on earth was all that about?' demanded Sue.

'Didn't you hear it?' cried Jinny, looking up so that Sue could see her white, panic-stricken face. 'Didn't you hear the hooves?'

'No. Only you galloping off like a lunatic.'

'Didn't you hear them coming from behind the stones? The hooves?'

'No, I did not. You must have heard Pippen. There must have been an echo or something that made it sound as if his hoofbeats were coming from that direction.'

Jinny remounted slowly. Her whole body ached. Her head throbbed.

'I know what Pippen sounds like,' she said. 'It wasn't Pippen.'

Six

'Now, you will be sensible and tell Miss Tuke that you'll be pleased to accept her offer,' insisted Jinny's mother.

Jinny was waiting for the Hortons to arrive and collect her for their day's pony trekking.

'You could look after her if you tried,' said Jinny reproachfully. 'I'd show you what to do, and, if anything did go wrong, Mr MacKenzie would come up and sort it out.'

'Oh, Jinny, be sensible. I could not look after Shantih. I know absolutely nothing about horses, and, although you never seem to notice it, there is a lot of work involved in keeping this house going. Miss Tuke is the ideal person to take her. There is no other solution.'

'There are always other ways. It's just that we haven't thought of them yet,' stated Jinny, straining her ears for the sound of the Hortons' car.

Mrs Manders sighed. 'Do you always have to be so difficult?' she asked.

Jinny didn't reply. She was thinking the same thing about her mother.

'Now, do tell Miss Tuke that you want her to take Shantih for the winter.'

'There's the Hortons,' cried Jinny in relief, jumping up and running out of the kitchen.

Mrs Manders stared after her. *If only the school at Inverburgh had been ready to open on time or I knew about horses*, she thought. *And she's looking like a ghost, having these nightmares every night.*

'Oh, Jinny, Jinny, Jinny,' Mrs Manders said aloud to the empty kitchen.

'Hi,' said Sue, opening the car door.

'Low,' said Jinny, climbing in beside her.

'You do look pale,' said Mrs Horton, inspecting Jinny. 'If you were Sue I'd say you were sickening for something.'

'I'm just low,' said Jinny. She hadn't slept much the night before. Not sleeping made it impossible to dream, and if she didn't dream, the Red Horse couldn't reach her. Jinny had spent the night sitting up in bed, reading. She had balanced two magazines on her head so that when she dozed off they fell down and woke her up again.

When they reached Miss Tuke's yard, six Highland ponies were standing tethered to a bar. There were three duns, one bay, one steel grey and one black pony.

'Bramble!' cried Jinny, and she was out of the car almost before it had stopped. She ran across the yard to the black pony. 'Bramble,' she called. 'There's the good pony. There's the good Bramble.'

The black pony turned his head, pricked his ears through his heavy forelock, wiffled his nostrils, uncertainly and knitted his brows together. He still wasn't sure who it was.

'Bramble,' called Jinny again, and the pony was certain. He whickered, flurries of sound to welcome Jinny.

'He knows you,' boomed Miss Tuke, striding across the yard. 'I've never seen him do that to anyone except myself. Pity you'll not need him again this winter. He must have enjoyed being with you.'

Jinny threw her arms round Bramble's neck. After Shantih, he was broad and bulky. Even his lips, fumbling at her hand for titbits, seemed rubbery and huge after Shantih's delicate lipping. Jinny ran her hand down his neck and over his back, and suddenly she was back to last winter, riding Bramble home from school, feeding him and grooming him.

'Dear Bramble,' said Jinny again. 'You would have been coming back to Finmory if only they'd finished the bloomin' school in time.'

Miss Tuke was welcoming the Hortons.

'Glad to see you haven't changed your minds,'

she said. 'You don't need to worry about a thing. All my ponies are patent safety. Absolutely guaranteed to look after the rawest recruit.'

'Not raw yet,' said Mr Horton, 'but I dare say I shall be before the day is over.'

'Mr and Mrs Cunningham,' said Miss Tuke, introducing a young man and woman.

'Tim and Marigold,' they said, introducing themselves.

Two other ladies joined them. One was very fat, with iron-grey hair and glasses. She introduced herself as Brenda, and her companion, who was round-shouldered with a vacant, worried expression, as Pam. All four were beginners who hadn't ridden before their trekking holiday.

'Normally,' said Miss Tuke, 'it is my unbreakable rule that every trekker has to groom and tack up their own pony.'

'Then we will not be leaving this yard,' declared Mrs Horton. 'I could never put that bit into a pony's mouth. Their teeth are so obviously built for biting.'

'Oh, Mummy,' muttered Sue.

'But,' continued Miss Tuke, 'since Mr and Mrs Horton are only with us for the day, I shall permit their daughter to help them.'

'Now,' she said, 'let's see – Marigold, Brenda and Pam, your mounts are in their boxes. When you've got them tacked up I'll check them for you. Tim, Beech for you.' Miss Tuke pointed to the bay pony that was tied to the rail.

'Mr Horton, Fergus for you.' She showed Mr Horton the biggest of the dun ponies. 'He is one hundred per cent shockproof. Compared to Fergus, your favourite armchair is dynamite.'

Mrs Horton was to ride Meg, the smallest of the duns, and Sue was to have Shona, the third dun.

'She'll nip you if she gets the chance,' Miss Tuke warned Sue. 'Too much darling pepperminting has been going on with her ladyship all summer. But she's a good ride. You'll enjoy her.'

Miss Tuke handed out dandy brushes, telling them to pay particular attention to where the saddle and girth would go.

'Have you seen my stables?' Miss Tuke asked Jinny.

'No.'

'Have a quick sortie round now, if you like.'

Jinny would rather have gone on grooming Bramble. She paused, trying to think of some way of saying 'no' politely, but Miss Tuke was already marching across the yard.

She only wants me to look round her stables so that I'll think they would be all right for Shantih, Jinny thought rebelliously, as she trailed after Miss Tuke.

'This is my tack room,' said Miss Tuke.

In spite of herself, Jinny was impressed. There were rows of saddle racks on the walls, each with a place for a bridle underneath it and the name of the pony to whom the tack belonged. There was a saddle horse, buckets, and a basket filled with tack-cleaning equipment. One wall was covered with the certificates Miss Tuke had won with her Highlands.

'And this is my feed house.'

It was as spruce and polished as the tack room. There was a neat row of feed bins, buckets with the ponies' names written on them hanging from hooks, and a sleek tabby cat licking her paws as she watched for mice.

'I have three boxes and six stalls,' said Miss Tuke, showing them to Jinny.

The boxes were occupied by a grey Highland, a skewbald, and a chestnut pony with a wall eye. Each pony had its attendant trekker working on it with a dandy.

'If you decide to let Shantih come here for the winter, she would have one of these boxes and probably a Highland next door to her for company.'

Jinny said nothing. She stood looking round the stabling. The floors of the boxes were well brushed, troughs scrubbed out, the woodwork freshly painted, but it wasn't the place for Shantih. The only place for Shantih was at Finmory, with Jinny there to look after her.

'It won't happen,' said Jinny. 'I'm not going to Duninver. I can't leave Shantih.'

'Let me know if you change your mind,' said Miss Tuke. 'I've taken quite a shine to her. Would stir up my middle-aged bones having her here.'

Jinny didn't want Miss Tuke to have taken a shine to her horse. She didn't want Shantih stirring up middle-aged bones.

'He will not stand still while I fasten his girth,' shrilled Pam. 'He is being a very naughty boy this morning.'

Miss Tuke went to her aid, and Jinny returned to Bramble.

Already Bramble was beginning to cast his summer coat and grow his dense winter one. Jinny swept her dandy brush down his strong neck and powerful shoulders and over his broad back. The familiar movements comforted her. So many mornings before she had set out for school she had groomed Bramble. She left his tail to the end. The hairs were coarse and wiry compared to Shantih's silken tail. Jinny felt she could have gone on trying to brush it out for hours without making much difference to it. Eventually she gave it up as a bad job and went to find his tack.

The yard was loud with voices.

'Darling, I cannot put that lump of metal into any creature's mouth. I am sure they can't like it,' pleaded Mrs Horton.

'Whoa there, Tiger,' cried Tim, as Beech whisked her tail. 'Got to be firm with them,' he informed Mr Horton.

'Let them know who's in charge.' Tim jumped hastily backwards as Beech shook her head.

'It's the size of this fellow that's worrying me,' confided Mr Horton. 'Do we ancients climb up steps, or is there a hoist to lower us into the saddle?'

'You spring, Daddy,' said Sue, tacking up Fergus for her father.

'I have not sprung anywhere for years,' said Mr Horton. 'I wonder might it be a better idea if I follow you in the car?'

'How are we doing?' asked Miss Tuke, distributing packed lunches in waterproof bags to be tied to the saddles. 'Getting on with it? Good, good. Jinny, would you saddle up the grey for me while I get the ladies on board. She's only four. Misty's her name. I'm riding her myself for a few treks this summer. She's still full of the joys, quite a handful. Only hope she's settled in by next year.'

When they were all mounted, Miss Tuke cast her experienced eye over her trekkers, untied Misty and heaved herself into the saddle. The young pony jumped back as Miss Tuke's weight banged down on her back.

'Stand still, you little varmit,' Miss Tuke shouted as she jabbed the pony in the mouth to stop it going forward while she hit it behind the saddle.

'Rattle up their ribs,' she announced. 'Always have a stick handy when you're riding a youngster.'

Jinny watched in silent despair. Would Miss Tuke

always have a stick handy when she was riding Shantih? If Miss Tuke tried to hit Shantih, the Arab would panic, but Miss Tuke would fight back. Jinny's heart sank as she watched Miss Tuke's heavy hands and her solid dead weight in the saddle. She would treat Shantih as if she were a trekking pony – shouting at her, hitting her, thumping down on her back and yanking at her mouth. No matter how smart the stables were or how spotless the feed house, Jinny knew that Shantih could never, ever come here.

'Everybody fit?' Miss Tuke called. 'Good. Mrs Horton come in front beside me. Mr Horton and Tim behind us. Marigold and Pam next. Brenda and Sue behind them. Jinny, you and Bramble are our rear guard. Pick up the drop offs and keep them all moving.'

'OK,' said Jinny. 'We'll do our best.'

'We're going to the white sands,' Miss Tuke told them. 'Bit further than we usually go, so let's hope the weather will be kind. The view is superb but the sands are mostly mud-coloured.'

Miss Tuke rode Misty out of the yard and Mrs Horton's pony fell in beside her.

'Here we go,' said Tim. 'Wagons roll. Keep Fergus up with me. He's Tiger's buddy.'

The three ladies, rather bunched together, their ponies glowering, went through the gate next, then Sue and Jinny.

The track from the yard led through Forestry roads,

then wound over hills that were grassy and more rolling than the moors around Finmory. Jinny smiled to herself. It was good to be riding Bramble again, to feel his steady stride and have his strong neck reaching in front of her.

'You are a good pony,' Jinny assured him, burying her hands in the warmth of his shaggy mane.

In front of them, the other trekkers bumped happily along. Brenda had her skewbald well under control. In spite of her fat she seemed to know what she was doing. Pam's chestnut had her well under control. Every now and again he stopped to restock with mouthfuls of grass.

'Let's try a trot,' called back Miss Tuke. 'Reins in one hand and a good tight hold on the front of the saddle with the other. Right? Good. Trek, trot forward.'

The ponies knew Miss Tuke's command. *I expect they trot here on every trek*, thought Jinny, watching the riders bumping about. *Bet the ponies would know where to trot even if there was no one riding them.*

'Hold on there,' encouraged Tim, as Mr Horton swooped dangerously to one side.

'Don't worry, I'm well anchored,' Mr Horton assured him. 'I'm holding the saddle with both hands.'

'Going to walk again,' called back Miss Tuke. 'Walk now.' But the ponies, hearing the shout, were already walking.

Jinny knew that, normally, trekking would have

bored her to death. She couldn't have bothered with so many beginners, would have wanted to canter and jump, but today she was glad they were all there. She wanted to be with a crowd of people, to be doing things together. The Red Horse could not reach her here. She was safe with the trekkers.

They had been riding for about two hours when the far glint of the sea came into sight and the track began to lead downhill.

'Lunch in half an hour,' called back Miss Tuke.

When they reached the shore, they tethered their ponies to stumps in the ground.

'There's a sheltered spot over here,' Miss Tuke told them, when she had checked that all the ponies were safely tied up. 'We can get behind those rocks. 'Fraid there isn't going to be a view today. You're out of luck.'

Black clouds were massing over the grey sky, and the waves rolling up the beach were white with foam.

Crouching in the shelter of the rocks, they ate their sandwiches and drank hot soup in paper cups from a thermos Miss Tuke had brought with her. The trekkers compared moments.

'Did you see Beech leap when that sheep got up suddenly?' asked Tim. 'I thought he was going in for the attack.'

'We call it shying,' said Miss Tuke. 'She was having you on. She has met a sheep before.'

Pam asked what she should do to stop her pony

grazing but no one heard her. Mr Horton said never again, and Mrs Horton said she was enjoying it and would be having shots on Pippen when she got home.

'We won't waste too much time here,' said Miss Tuke, brisking them up. 'No point in hanging around when there's no view. Think we're in for a soaking and we've a fair bit to go.'

'Mercy, woman,' said Mr Horton. 'Let me have a few more moments of earth-bound bliss before I go into orbit again. I am an old man.'

But Miss Tuke was worried about the weather, and chased them back to the ponies as soon as possible.

Quickly and efficiently she helped the trekkers to untie their ponies and tighten their girths, then she hoisted them into their saddles before they realised what was happening.

Despite Miss Tuke's haste, heavy raindrops were falling as they rode away from the shore.

'Into single file here,' Miss Tuke told them in her foghorn voice. 'Keep directly behind the pony in front of you. There are a lot of rabbit warrens here, so don't let them wander about. Pam, shorten your reins and sit back a bit. Don't let him graze.'

Although the sky was black and louring, it still wasn't really raining – only heavy, single drops of rain. In front of Jinny, the trekkers were billowing into plastic macs and rainhoods, making a bright patch of colour on the bleak moor.

'Why can't we have a trot?' asked Sue, riding beside Jinny. 'We'd be home much more quickly if she let us trot.'

Jinny hunched her shoulders. 'Expect it would be slower if one of them fell off,' she said.

Really, she didn't care what happened to the trekkers. All the impossible things had come crowding back into her mind. It was not possible that in a fortnight Shantih would be at Miss Tuke's and she would be at Duninver School.

What am I doing here? thought Jinny furiously. *I should be riding Shantih. I should be finding someone in Glenbost who will look after her through the week. I should be making money. I shouldn't be wasting my time here.*

Then Jinny glanced back over her shoulder, saw white mist wreathing between the moor and the clouds, mists sweeping over the heather towards them, white fingers reaching out to grasp them, ghosts rising. And Jinny knew why she was there – to be with other people, to be doing something safe and ordinary, to be where the Red Horse couldn't find her. She had been safe in the morning, had almost forgotten the Horse, but now, with the change in the weather, the Horse was close behind her, was all about her, seeking her out.

Suddenly the wind whipped a plastic rainhood off Marigold's head and sent it flapping down the line of ponies. Brenda grabbed at it and missed. Her sudden movement startled her pony, who leaped forward into the rear of Pam's pony. The rainhood blew into Meg's quarters. The terrified pony bucked and Mrs Horton screamed and clutched.

'Hands down,' shouted Miss Tuke, but her words were lost as the plastic rainhood came crackling and blustering straight at her pony's head. The young pony reared in fright.

Jinny urged Bramble forward, knowing that if Miss Tuke's young pony started playing up, all the ponies would become excited. At that moment a sheet of lightning flickered over the sky and, almost immediately, thunder crashed over their heads.

'Hold onto your saddles,' instructed Miss Tuke, unable to do any more than call out instructions as she struggled to calm her own terrified pony.

Jinny saw Fergus charge forward with Mr Horton clinging to the saddle, his plastic mac billowing out in the wind. Tim and Beech were close behind him, and in a second it seemed that the whole trek was galloping over the moor. Jinny fought to hold Bramble back, to steady him, to stop him joining in the runaway.

The storm clouds burst open. Rain blew into Jinny's face, blinding her; the wind howled in her ears, deafening her, and Bramble fought to follow the others.

And then the plastic-coated trekkers had gone. Jinny shouted aloud, the sound she made came from the base of her throat, blood-curdling, haunting. Her heels drummed against her pony's sides as she urged him forward, forced him straight through the band of galloping riders. Again and again Jinny cried out, rallying those who followed her to ride faster. They crouched over their ponies' necks, the skins they wore were sodden with the rain, their long hair matted on their shoulders. Their wordless cry spread over the moors, flowed out behind them and Jinny was one of them. She rode with the Pony Folk.

'Jinny Manders. Come back here. Stop galloping. Stop it at once.'

Miss Tuke's furious voice reached Jinny. Her hands gripped leather reins again, once more she was riding on a saddle. For moments she was lost, terrified, caught in the horror of not knowing where she was, who she was.

'Stop that galloping!'

Somehow, Jinny swung her pony back to the sound of the voice. The moor was dotted with loose ponies and trekkers lying on the ground.

'What do you think you're doing, forcing him on like that? You could easily have stopped Bramble.'

Jinny rubbed her hand over her eyes.

'Where have they gone?' she demanded. 'The Pony Folk?'

Jinny searched the moor for the dark galloping fury, the men crouching over the necks of their ponies, the beat and pound of their hooves.

'Where have they gone?' Jinny cried.

$\mathcal{S}$*even*

The next morning, Jinny was sitting in the back of their car, being driven home from Inverburgh to Finmory. The seat next to her father was empty, but somehow it was safer to be sitting in the back and better for talking to her father. She could say things to the back of his head that she couldn't have said if she had been able to see his expression.

'There must be someone around here who has a university degree and a teaching whatever-it-is-they-need. MUST be. Please, Daddy. We could put an advert in the paper and I could go to them every day for lessons. I'd learn more that way. Being the only one, I'd learn much more. But honestly it doesn't matter. Artists don't need to go to school. We only need to be allowed to draw and paint. That's all.'

Mr Manders' back remained utterly unmoved.

Jinny knew that really he wasn't listening to her.

'Please, please try to understand. I can't leave Shantih.'

'You won't be leaving her. I've promised to take you over to Miss Tuke's every weekend so you can ride her.'

'She won't be mine anymore. Miss Tuke will ruin her, banging about on top of her. She'll not be the same. She'll think I've left her. How would you like it if you had to leave Mummy? Never see her all week? You wouldn't like that.'

'Oh, Jinny, try to be sensible. Shantih is only a horse.'

'How can you even think that?' demanded Jinny bitterly. If her father thought that, there didn't seem to be much point in going on arguing with him. Jinny stared despondently out of the car window.

As if Shantih were any ordinary horse, she thought. To Jinny, Shantih was a golden horse, she dazzled in Jinny's imagination – a horse of the sun – and Jinny loved her more than she loved herself.

They had taken Ken to Nell Storr's, and Mrs Manders and Petra to Inverburgh station to catch the Glasgow train. Petra's piano exam was on Saturday morning. Going to Glasgow today, they would spend the night in a hotel and catch a train back to Inverburgh on Saturday afternoon.

Petra had been cool and confident, her case packed by Thursday morning, certain she had everything with her, not having to check over and over again the way

Jinny would have had to do. Even her good luck black cat was neatly packed in its own little box. *Not that Petra needed good luck; she was prepared*, thought Jinny.

Nell Storr had been waiting for Ken, sitting outside her shop at the wheel of her sports car. Watching them drive off, Jinny had wished that she could have gone with them, that someone had seen her drawings and had wanted to meet her. She had wanted to escape from Finmory. Surely, if she had been driving to London, the Red Horse couldn't have followed her, and in the excitement of London she might have forgotten some of the things that Miss Tuke had said to her. Mr Horton had twisted his ankle, Tim had broken his collar bone and Brenda had refused to get onto her pony again. Miss Tuke had held Jinny responsible for the runaway and Mr Horton had been furious with her.

'It was the lightning that scared them and Marigold's rainhood,' Jinny had protested.

'If you had controlled Bramble, as you could have done quite easily, none of it would have happened,' Miss Tuke had insisted. 'You knew I was riding a young pony. I could do nothing. But for you to go urging Bramble on, yelling like that and charging through them all! I am disgusted with you.'

And there had been nothing more that Jinny could have said to defend herself. She couldn't have started to try to explain to Miss Tuke that while she had been galloping and yelling she hadn't been with the trekkers. She had been surrounded by the small dark riders, had ridden with the Pony Folk from the past, her voice mingling with their cries, Bramble's hoofbeats had been part of their long silent stampede. Even standing in Miss Tuke's yard when it was all over, the wild, hawk screams of the dark riders still filled her head.

'I *am* sorry,' Jinny had said.

'Sorry won't mend Tim's collar bone or Mr Horton's ankle,' Miss Tuke had told her, and Jinny had said no more. There was nothing more she could say.

Mr Manders parked the car in front of Finmory. They got out and went inside through the iron-studded front door. Standing in the hall, the empty house seemed suddenly menacing, with its high ceilings and shadowy corridors. Kelly came through from the kitchen and, for a second, Jinny didn't see him as a tail-wagging, welcoming dog. She saw a grey wolf skulking in the shadows, its yellow eyes fixed unblinkingly on her face. Jinny shrieked with sudden fear.

'Whatever is the matter?' demanded her father, and Kelly was dog again.

'Nothing,' Jinny muttered, stroking Kelly, ashamed at being so silly.

Yet she was afraid. No amount of pretending that she wasn't could make any difference. In her bedroom, the mural of the Red Horse waited for her and, outside the house, the wilderness of moorland waited for the darkness that would set the Red Horse free, to let it come raging into her dreams. All day they would be going on digging at Brachan, disturbing the things that had lain hidden for hundreds of years. Jinny shivered uncontrollably.

Now there was only herself and her father left. The others had gone just when she needed them most. Jinny clutched desperately at her father's arm.

'You won't go too?' she cried. 'You won't leave me alone here? I can't stay here alone.'

'Of course I'm not going,' said Mr Manders. 'What is wrong, Jinny? What is upsetting you like this? It's more than being worried about Shantih, isn't it?'

Mr Manders looked down anxiously at his daughter's pinched face, her panic-filled eyes. The weight of her long hair made her face seem sharper and more drawn than ever.

'Can't you tell me what's wrong?'

But Jinny couldn't. She couldn't start to try and tell her father about her dreams of the Red Horse, how, when she was dreaming, it was more real than being awake. She shook her head dumbly.

'You won't go, will you? Promise?'

'Is it likely?' said Mr Manders. 'Look, go and make us both a mug of coffee and then come into the pottery and decorate some tiles for me.'

'I'm going to jump Shantih,' Jinny said.

'Make the coffee first?'

'OK.'

Jinny went through to the kitchen. She filled the kettle and put milk and coffee into two mugs. A gull flew across the window. The sweep of its wings, the suddenness of its moving shadow, made Jinny spring back, her heart thumping.

'It's only a bird. It's only a bird. Stop being so silly. Stop it!' Jinny told herself. 'It couldn't happen. I couldn't be left alone here because I wouldn't stay here. I'd sleep with Sue, or go into Glenbost and spend the night with Dolina, or to the MacKenzies. I wouldn't stay here, so it can't happen.'

Jinny poured boiling water into the mugs, and was about to call her father when the phone rang – shrill, commanding. Jinny froze, the kettle still in her hand, as she listened to her father's footsteps hurrying to answer the phone. She heard him lift the receiver and give their number.

Jinny could only hear half of the conversation, but she knew at once from her father's voice that the phone call was something special. As he spoke, his replies grew louder and more excited.

'But I don't believe it! I absolutely don't believe it,' he cried.

'How tremendous.'

'Yes, yes. Of course.'

'Certainly.'

'At once?'

'Of course, I do appreciate the urgency.'

'Could I phone you back? Yes, in about five minutes.'

'Yes. Yes.'

'I'll let you know at once, but, to be quite truthful, I still do not believe it possible.'

Mr Manders put the phone down with a bang. He came running into the kitchen, grabbed Jinny by the waist and danced her round the kitchen.

'It's my book,' he cried as they whirled round. 'They actually want to publish it. And not only that, they're rushing it through, bringing it out in three months!' Mr Manders released Jinny and fell back spreadeagled into one of the kitchen chairs.

'Fantastic,' cried Jinny. 'Absolutely super. You're an author now. A real author!' She was fizzing over at her father's success. 'Wait till Mum hears about it.'

'There's only one thing,' said Mr Manders, and Jinny felt a cold clutch of fear tighten in her stomach.

'What?' she demanded, when her father paused.

'Well,' said Mr Manders, standing up and reaching for his mug of coffee, 'all the rush is because there's a report coming out in three months about the problem of unemployed school leavers. A lot of my book is about this and they want to link up my book with the report.'

'But that's good, isn't it?'

'They're hoping for a TV documentary based on the

report and the solutions I suggest in my book. If they can get it fixed up it should make quite a difference to the money the book brings in.'

'That's even better,' said Jinny, still not able to understand what was troubling her father.

'The TV producer who might be interested in doing the documentary is having dinner with the publisher tonight, and they want me to fly down to London this afternoon so I can meet them all.'

Jinny felt as if she was choking for breath. Her lungs had stopped working. She wanted to yell, 'You can't! You can't! You can't leave me here alone!'

'Seems vital that we get in first with my ideas before anyone else gets wind of the project. I'd be back tomorrow – but what about tonight? You would need to stay here.'

'Of course I can stay here,' declared Jinny, her voice too loud, too high-pitched. 'I'll stay with Sue, share her tent. Of course you must go.'

Jinny saw relief smooth out her father's face.

'Are you sure you would be all right with the Hortons?' he said.

'Perfectly all right,' replied Jinny. She was gulping down mouthfuls of burning-hot coffee to stop herself crying. It had been so sudden. Yet somehow she had known it must happen. 'I'll go and ask them now. I'm sure it will be OK.'

Jinny caught Shantih and rode bareback to the

Horton's tent. It had happened. They were leaving her alone. All her family leaving her alone when she needed them most. Now there was no one left to protect her from the Red Horse.

Sue had seen her and came out of the tent to meet her.

'Hi,' she said. 'Have they all gone?'

'How did you know,' demanded Jinny.

'Because you told me. Ken to London, and Petra and your mother to Glasgow.'

'Dad's going too,' said Jinny. 'To London. He had a phone call from the publisher and they are going to publish his book.'

'Good for him,' said Sue.

'They want him to fly to London this afternoon to meet a TV producer.'

'TV as well!' exclaimed Sue.

'So can I stay with you. Just for tonight.'

'There'll be no one left at Finmory?'

'No, so please can I share with you?'

''Course you can. I'll just tell Mum and Dad.'

Waiting outside on Shantih, Jinny couldn't quite make out what Sue was saying, only hear the voices inside the tent.

'That's fixed,' said Sue, coming out again. 'They're dead pleased about your father's book. Say to give him their congratulations.'

'Thanks,' said Jinny.

'Come over when he's gone,' said Sue. 'We can jump.'

'Will do,' said Jinny, riding away.

For a moment she couldn't help thinking that there had been something odd about Sue when she had come back out of the tent. Normally when Sue spoke to you she looked you straight in the eye, but just now she had been avoiding Jinny's gaze.

Maybe she doesn't want me, Jinny thought, but it didn't make any difference, she wasn't staying alone in Finmory. For the first time since they had come to live there, Finmory wasn't home. No one was left there now. Only the Red Horse.

'I can stay with Sue,' Jinny told her father.

'Grand,' said her father. 'Thank you. I'll phone them and let them know.'

'There's a flight leaving at three-thirty,' Mr Manders said when he came off the phone. 'I'll be straight back tomorrow morning. I'll phone your mother and Petra from London. Tell them the good news.'

Jinny nodded, trying to make herself smile, not wanting to spoil her father's success.

It's so unfair, she thought. *Why has it to be like this? Why couldn't we all have been here? Why should it happen now? Why?*

And clear into Jinny's head came a picture of the dig at Brachan. She saw the scarred hillside, the archaeologists with their measuring rods and graph paper. All busy, but not one of them knowing what they were doing.

Jinny shook her head, trying to clear it. *What's wrong?* she thought. *Why do I keep getting mixed up? Seeing things that aren't there? Saying things and then not knowing what I mean. Perhaps I'm going mad. I'm so worried about Shantih I'm going mad, but nobody cares.*

Again Jinny saw the dig in her mind's eye. This time, the archaeologist's had bland sheep's faces. They were passing some small metal object from hand to hand and their hands were like claws. As Jinny stood by the table in Finmory's kitchen, she saw the grey shapes of wolves coming out of the disturbed earth. Then, as the picture in her head grew clearer, she saw that they weren't wolves, they were the small dark men she had ridden with yesterday; men dressed in wolfskins, with the wolf masks pulled over their heads. They crept closer to the archaeologists and, behind them, the sky grew red.

At first Jinny thought they were going to attack, and then several of them turned and looked directly at her. The wolf heads they wore didn't cover their faces and Jinny could see their expressions quite clearly. To her surprise they were not savage at all, but gentle, almost sad, as if they were being forced to watch some tragedy and were helpless to prevent it happening. Then it seemed to Jinny that they wanted to speak to her but couldn't. As if they needed her help.

'Jinny, what is the matter?' demanded Mr Manders. 'You look as if you've seen a ghost. What is wrong?'

Jinny blinked her way back to the kitchen. Desperately she wanted to fling herself into her father's arms, to plead with him not to leave her alone, to tell him about her nightmares. But she couldn't. If she made a fuss he wouldn't go to London.

Anyway, he wouldn't really understand, Jinny thought. *No one else can help me. Whatever happens is going to happen to me.*

So she only said, 'Oh nothing. I was daydreaming.' And Mr Manders, not wanting to interfere too much, didn't ask any more questions.

''Bye,' shouted Jinny, waving to her father as he started up the car. 'Good luck.'

'Take care of yourself,' called back Mr Manders. 'Go straight to the Hortons and I'll be back tomorrow as soon as I can.'

'Will do,' Jinny shouted back. ''Bye.'

She stood at the front door, watching the car disappear down the drive, stood listening until the sound of its engine faded into silence. She was alone.

Jinny shut the front door and stood in the hall. In the silence, the whole house seemed to be listening to her breathing. There was the creak of a door being pushed open, and Kelly came padding towards her. He lay down beside her, watching her from under his thatch of grey hair.

Jinny made a dash for the stairs, ran up them, raced along the landing and up the ladder of stairs to her own room. Taking care not to look at the Horse, Jinny found her canvas bag, stuffed a nightdress and a heavy sweater into it. She dragged her sleeping bag from the bottom of her wardrobe and ran back down to the bathroom. She added her toilet things to her canvas bag and tore down to the kitchen. She locked the back door, fumbling in her haste, feeling the eyes of the unseen watchers staring from corners and from behind closed doors. She sped back through the hall, grabbed Kelly by the scruff of his neck and bundled him outside. Turning, Jinny pulled the front door shut and locked it securely. She dropped the key into her canvas bag.

'There,' she said aloud. 'That's it. I'm not going back in there until everyone is home again.'

Kelly had twisted free from Jinny's grasp. He sat and watched her running down the path to Shantih's field. When she was out of sight he settled down on the doorstep, waiting for her to come back.

Eight

Sue was schooling Pippen. She rode to the field gate when she saw Jinny approaching.

'Do you want to jump?'

'Yes,' said Jinny in surprise. She had been expecting Sue to want to ride over the moors, or at least suggest that they should go down to the bay.

'Better change the jumps, then,' Sue said, leaping off Pippen. 'They could jump this lot backwards and still have a clear round, they know them so well.'

'Let's build a proper course,' agreed Jinny enthusiastically. Jumping was the only thing that might take her mind off the Red Horse. She slid to the ground and looked round at the tumbledown pile of the jumps. 'We were going to do it days ago, before everything was messed up. Really, we need to start all over again. This lot have had it.'

'We'll build a complete new course and then we'll have a competition over it,' said Sue. 'Take their tack off and let them graze while we course-build.'

'Right,' agreed Jinny, and began to loosen Shantih's girths. Then she stopped, and pulled them tight again. 'I'll take my sleeping bag and things down to the tent first,' she said.

'Oh, don't do that,' cried Sue. 'Keep them here. Don't go trailing down to the tent just now.'

Jinny looked suspiciously at Sue. She didn't think a few minutes would make any difference.

'Look, hang your bag from the gatepost and stick your sleeping bag between the bars. There, that's OK, isn't it? Now come on.'

They took off their horses' tack and turned them loose. Shantih broke away from Jinny at a springing trot. She went straight to the corner of the field closest to the moors and began to race up and down the hedge, whinnying.

'She gets so excited,' said Jinny, watching her horse in case she tried to break out. 'Perhaps she remembers when she was shut in Mr MacKenzie's yard with his Shetlands.'

'She'll settle. She'll not leave Pippen,' said Sue, watching her pony's placid grazing.

'Hope so,' said Jinny as she stared at Shantih, thinking, as she always did when Shantih was misbehaving, how beautiful the Arab was. *Miss Tuke won't see it like that*, thought Jinny. *Miss Tuke will make Shantih behave herself.*

'Come on, let's move these first,' said Sue, starting to haul the scattered wooden boxes into a pile at the side of the field. Jinny went to help her. 'We want to build them with a good spread on them, and not make them any higher,' said Sue, organising.

'Not too low,' said Jinny. 'Shall we have a double and a triple? Shantih's never jumped anything like that.'

'Clear everything away first and then we can start from scratch. Plan it out properly.'

They dragged the straw bales, bits of broken sheep pen, the heather-filled sacks, the four rusted cans, the poles and the wooden fish boxes into the side of the field.

'Shall we go and scrounge round the yard?' asked Jinny. 'Mr MacKenzie said we weren't to take his good gate, but we could have the hen coop. Expect there'll be other things we could take as well.'

'Right,' said Sue.

'Can we take the hen coop?' Jinny asked Mr MacKenzie, who was turning over his midden.

'Aye,' he said. 'As long as you're putting it all back behind the hay shed when you've finished with your nonsense.'

'When they choose me to jump for Britain and interview me on the telly, I shall mention your name,' Jinny promised.

Mr MacKenzie snorted. 'Just be clearing the field, that will do me well enough,' he assured her. 'And where would your father be off to?'

Jinny explained.

'That will just leave yourself in the house then?'

'I'm staying . . .' began Jinny.

'Isn't that Shantih?' interrupted Sue. 'It sounded as if she was trying to break out.'

'It would not surprise me,' said Mr MacKenzie. 'It's not the peaceable bone she has in the whole of her body.'

'I can't hear her,' said Jinny, listening.

'I did,' said Sue. 'Let's get back.'

They hurried back to the field, carrying the hen coop, a broken deckchair and four more fish boxes.

Although Shantih was still trotting up and down the hedge, she didn't seem any more disturbed than when they had left her.

'Must have been wrong,' said Sue, and Jinny wondered why she had been in such a hurry to get away from Mr MacKenzie.

Almost as if she didn't want him to know that I was spending the night in their tent, Jinny thought.

'Do you want to try a triple?' Sue asked.

'Oh yes,' said Jinny, going to help her.

'We'll start at this end,' said Sue. 'Go down that side first, over an easy jump, up the other side over a triple, and back down the middle over a big jump.'

'Puissance,' said Jinny, forcing everything else except the thought of jumping Shantih out of her mind. 'Enormous jumps.'

They made the first jump out of the hen coop and the heather-filled sacks. The first two parts of the triple they built out of poles, and the third part out of the deckchair, boxes and straw bales. The jump in the middle was built out of all that they had left.

'Not very professional,' said Sue regretfully.

'Suppose not,' agreed Jinny, 'but it is pretty good. I expect all the top showjumpers have practice jumps at home that look something like these. I've seen photographs of them in books.'

'Better school first,' Sue said, when they were mounted again.

Jinny didn't want to be bothered. Reluctantly, she rode Shantih round behind Pippen as he trotted and cantered figures of eight.

Shantih was annoyed at being caught again and taken away from her hedge. She threatened to buck, hitching her quarters, shying suddenly and stopping stock-still to stare goggle-eyed across the moors, blaring out her trumpeting whinnies. Jinny knew that if Pippen hadn't been there in front of her, Shantih would have been bucking and rearing in earnest.

'Can't we jump now?' Jinny demanded. 'All this messing about is driving Shantih crazy.'

'Sorry. Shall I go first, in case you crash through?'

Jinny nodded, and Sue rode Pippen at the first jump. He cantered up to it and popped neatly over it, but despite Sue's aids he stopped at the first part of the triple.

'He always does that. He has to put his glasses on to make sure there really are three jumps. Now he'll jump it without any fuss.'

Sue turned Pippen and rode him at the triple again; this time he bounced over the jumps like a rubber ball. He cantered round the top of the field and up over the heap jump with a neat bound.

Jinny had been struggling to hold Shantih back. Now she half reared, snatched at the bit and charged forward. Jinny couldn't hold her. It was all she could do to steer her at the first jump. Yards in front of it, Shantih sailed into the air, soared over the boxes, touched down far beyond them and, with her head low, hooves drumming, she went battering round to face the triple. Jinny knew they were going much too fast, but she didn't care. She wanted the speed, wanted to go even faster.

'Slow her down for the triple,' yelled Sue. 'Jinny, slow her down. Don't try to jump it at that speed.'

Shantih rose at the triple as if it had been a single jump. Jinny had done nothing to try and check her. She sat balanced easily over her horse's withers, her knees tight against the saddle, her hands light on the reins. She felt Shantih's surprise as she rose over the first jump and saw the next jump so close to the first. She felt Shantih stretch herself in mid air trying to clear the first two parts of the triple in one jump.

'Go on, Shantih, go on,' Jinny cried and then knew that Shantih couldn't possibly clear the first two jumps; knew they were going to fall.

Shantih's hind legs caught in the poles of the second jump, bringing her down. Jinny was thrown into the ground in front of the straw bales. She lay there helplessly, watching Shantih struggling to stand. Saw her surge upright and trot away with her stirrups dangling and her reins around her legs.

'You stupid idiot,' cried Sue furiously as Jinny tried to stand up, felt her head swimming, and sat down hard on the straw bales. 'That was all your own fault. You didn't even try to slow her down. You were kicking her on. I saw you.'

Jinny felt dizzy. She put her head down between her legs, knowing that what Sue was saying was true. She had wanted Shantih to go faster so that she could escape from the Horse.

'You should think yourself lucky that she hasn't hurt herself,' said Sue.

Hazily, Jinny got to her feet, found her hard hat, which had come off, stuck it firmly back on her head and went unsteadily to catch Shantih.

'Now,' said Sue, when Jinny had remounted, 'keep her trotting and take her over the triple again. I've squashed it down a bit.'

Still feeling decidedly hazy, Jinny rode Shantih at the triple. She kept her at a trot and Shantih leaped stiffly over the first part, then crashed her way through the other two jumps, scattering poles and straw bales about the field.

'Try again,' said Sue, rebuilding the triple. 'Canter her in a circle first.'

This time, Shantih demolished all three jumps.

'If I let her gallop she'll jump them, now she knows there are three of them,' said Jinny, hating to see Shantih knocking down the jumps.

'Have you ever ridden her over cavalletti?' asked Sue.

'You know I haven't,' said Jinny crossly. 'You know I never did any jumping until you came this summer.'

The light was fading into the grey of late afternoon. Although Jinny was hardly conscious of it, part of her knew the day was beginning to die, the night was coming closer.

Sue laid four poles on the ground for Shantih to trot over. She mounted Pippen and rode over the poles herself to show Jinny how Pippen could trot neatly between the poles without touching them.

'Once she can do that,' said Sue, 'we'll put up a low jump after the last pole. That will teach her not to get so excited.'

Shantih reared impatiently while Jinny tried to listen to Sue's Pony Club instruction. When Jinny did ride

Shantih over the poles, she clattered them all and galloped off.

At first Jinny really tried to listen to Sue and do what she told her, but the early evening was growing darker. The massed bulk of the mountains were being swallowed up by the grey light. Stray drifts of mist breathed over the moor.

'I think she's had enough,' said Jinny at last. 'She's only making a worse mess of it every time we do it. I'll take her over to her field then come back to your tent.'

'Oh no,' said Sue quickly. 'It's far too early for that. I'll ride Pippen over with you.'

'But I've got my sleeping bag and things here,' objected Jinny. 'I thought you could take them to your tent for me.'

'I'll take them with us on Pippen,' said Sue. 'No trouble. He won't mind.' And before Jinny could stop her, Sue had fixed Jinny's sleeping bag onto Pippen's saddle and slung Jinny's canvas bag over her shoulder. 'Right. Off we go,' Sue said, riding to the gate.

When they reached Finmory, Jinny took Shantih into her box to feed her.

'I'll put Pippen in a stall,' said Sue. 'No point in standing here holding him. In fact, no point in waiting here while Shantih's taking years to eat her nuts. Let's go into the house and have a drink of lemonade.'

'But I'm coming to stay with you,' said Jinny, the

panic she felt sounding in her voice. 'You're not coming to Finmory.'

'Of course,' said Sue, 'if you don't want to give me a drink of lemonade, that's OK.'

'It's not worth it,' said Jinny.

'She'll be ten more minutes eating those nuts and I've spent most of the afternoon instructing you. I need a lemonade.'

'We'll get it in your tent,' insisted Jinny, willing Shantih to eat her nuts more quickly.

'But we're here now. Come on. Don't be so mean.'

The last thing Jinny wanted to do was to go back into Finmory. It's grey stone walls looked menacing and gaunt against the backdrop of mist. The blank windows seemed dead and cold.

'Well, just say if you don't want to give me a lemonade,' insisted Sue.

Jinny glowered. 'It's not worth it,' she said again.

'Oh, don't be so feeble. Come on now. We've plenty of time. We don't need to go back to our tent until eightish. Stop being so mean.'

'Shantih's nearly finished her feed. In fact, that will be enough for her.'

'Then let's put them both in your field and have tea at Finmory.'

Jinny wanted to shout, 'No! No! No! I'm not going back to Finmory, not until all my family are there. I'm not going back again.'

But she was too tired to go on arguing with Sue. She leaned against the box door and watched Shantih finishing off the remains of her feed. 'Well, if you really want to . . .' she said.

'It'll be fun,' said Sue. 'Let's put them in your field and have tea at Finmory.'

'Lemonade,' said Jinny, 'and then we're going to your tent.'

They turned Pippen and Shantih out into the field, and Sue bustled Jinny along the path to Finmory.

Pretend you've lost the key, suggested a voice in Jinny's head, but somehow she couldn't. She fished the key out of her bag and pushed open the front door. Kelly walked in at her heels.

'You are lucky,' exclaimed Sue, 'living here. Ours is a bungalow, in a row of bungalows all exactly the same. I'll bet there's not another house the same as Finmory.'

But Jinny wasn't listening. She was too busy switching on lights to banish the shadows.

'I'll make the tea,' said Sue. 'What would you like? Scrambled egg?'

Jinny sat down at the kitchen table. Her head ached where she had knocked it when she came off.

'I thought you only wanted a lemonade,' she muttered, but already Sue was breaking eggs into a bowl.

Jinny watched, her ears peeled for the least sound.

The creak of a floorboard, the squeak of a loose window frame, the stir of a curtain made the skin creep on the nape of her neck. She was listening for the sound of hooves, the brazen whinny.

'Grub up,' beamed Sue, handing her a plate of scrambled egg and tomatoes. 'Eat up.'

'Then we're going to your tent,' stated Jinny.

Sue didn't reply.

'We are,' said Jinny, and ate her scrambled egg between two slices of bread, the way she wasn't allowed to when her mother was there. Munching her sandwich, Jinny tried to imagine where her family would be at that particular moment, but to her dismay she had not a clear idea of where any of them were. They had all vanished.

'Isn't this super,' beamed Sue. 'The mist outside makes it even better in here.'

Jinny was gulping down the last of her sandwich.

'Listen,' said Sue. 'Do let's stay here tonight. It would be a real adventure. Just us.'

'No!' cried Jinny. 'No! We're going back to your tent.'

'There's no adventure in that. You can come and stay in the tent tomorrow night if you want to. But tonight we can be here. No one to tell us what to do. We can go to bed when we like.'

'No!'

Sue looked carefully at Jinny. 'What's wrong with you?' she asked. 'First you don't even want to come back for a lemonade, and now, when we've the chance of a super adventure on our own, you want to go running back to my mum and dad. I think you're scared.'

'Of course I'm not.' Jinny hotly denied the accusation.

'You're a coward, Jinny.'

'I am not!' cried Jinny, wondering how anyone could say such a thing, actually say it to another person.

'Then let's stay here.'

Suddenly Jinny felt too weary to argue. A strange numbness held her there, made her unable to fight with Sue. It was like the moments in the dentist's waiting room when it was still possible to pretend that she was going to be suddenly sick, or dash out screaming, or just refuse to go into the surgery because she couldn't bear the drill. But she never did. She knew she had to have her tooth filled and she just sat there, waiting for it to happen. Now that she had come back into Finmory, she couldn't escape again. She just sat, elbows on the kitchen table, chin propped on her hands, listening to Sue's bubbling enthusiasm.

'We could make toffee and eat it hot, or have a midnight feast,' enthused Sue. 'Jinny, it'll be great.'

But Jinny was drawn to something else that stirred in the house, something else that was waiting for her, that had known she would come back.

'You'll need to tell your parents that you're staying here,' Jinny's voice was flat, the words difficult to put together.

'Well, actually,' said Sue. 'I don't need to, because they know. I didn't know how to tell you, but Dad's still pretty mad about his ankle, and he says he's hurt his back as well. He seemed to think it was you galloping past that made him fall off.'

Jinny looked down guiltily, fiddling with her knife.

'It isn't that they didn't want to have you,' went on Sue, 'but there's not very much room in the tent, and when Mummy said why didn't I come and spend the night with you here, it seemed the best thing to do. And I did so want to stay at Finmory. I've always wanted to live in a house like this. You don't mind, do you?'

In a way, Jinny wasn't surprised. In a way she had known that she had never had any choice. She had to stay at Finmory tonight.

Later in the evening, they checked on their horses. They were both in Shantih's field. Pippen was grazing – stolid, clockwork – while Shantih stood at the corner of the field closest to the moors. Her every muscle was tense, her neck arched and her head poised. As the girls approached, she flung herself away from them, stormed in a sudden gallop around the field, mane and tail streaming about her, and then went back to her watching, her frozen staring out over the moonlit moors.

Jinny shut Finmory's heavy front door. It creaked and groaned, its wood swollen by the mist. The key grated in the lock as Jinny turned it.

'There,' said Sue. 'That's us safe for the night.'

Jinny could only think that if something was looking for her, now it would know where to find her.

By half-past twelve, Sue admitted to being tired enough to want to go to bed. They filled hot-water bottles and drank final mugs of chocolate.

'Goodnight,' Sue said, going into the spare room. 'Sleep well. We'll do more cavalletti tomorrow.'

'Goodnight,' said Jinny. Tomorrow morning seemed thousands and thousands of years away.

She walked along the landing, keeping herself close and tight. Not looking at the shadowy doorways, turning her head away from the windows, clenching her teeth.

At Petra's bedroom door she stopped, and went in. It was all neat and tidy. Petra's white and pink bedspread, her flowery nightdress case, the pink frill round her dressing table, were all controlled and tame.

I could sleep here, Jinny thought. *I'd be safe here. I could spend the night in Petra's room and I'd wake up in the morning and nothing would have happened.*

But she went back out onto the landing and walked slowly towards the stairs that led to her room. The grey shape of Kelly padded behind her.

Nine

The Red Horse on Jinny's mural glowed through the silvery moonlight. Instead of avoiding the mural, as she had done on other nights, Jinny went and stood in front of it. Standing perfectly still, she looked quietly at it.

'Only a painting,' she told herself. 'Why am I afraid of it?'

Petra would say it was all a nonsense, that, as usual, Jinny had let her imagination get out of control. Jinny knew that it wasn't that. There had always been a strangeness about the painting, something that Jinny hadn't been able to understand.

She wondered who the tinker girl had been who had come to paint the Red Horse. *Here, in this very room,* Jinny thought, *with Mr MacKenzie a boy, younger than me, sitting watching her*.

As Jinny stared, the Horse seemed to grow – its

yellow eyes burning, its charging hooves pressed on the edge of movement. Jinny stood still, held by the power of the painting. She could not move, only wait for the horse to gallop from the wall.

Kelly stood up, came stiff-legged from where he had been lying by the window, to stand beside Jinny. He pushed his grey head against her leg, licked at her hand. The spell that had held Jinny motionless was broken. The mural was only a painting once again.

Jinny shuddered. She paused for a second to glance through the window at the streamers of mist, floating, diaphanous drifts of vapour, flowing down the mountains, breathing over the moors, then she flung herself through to the other half of her room and stared over the garden to Shantih's field.

Pippen was a black mass of shadow lying by the hedge, while Shantih was still staring out across the moors. The sea was quicksilver, chequered by the cloud shadows as they swept across the moon.

Jinny sat on the edge of the bed. She was afraid to sleep. It seemed that all the things that belonged to her everyday life were no longer important, were toys put away in a toy box, and whatever it was that she was waiting for was the only real thing.

I'm not going to sleep. I'm not, Jinny told herself, but her eyes wouldn't stay open. She had to lie down on her bed.

'But not to sleep,' she murmured, 'not to . . .'

The black marsh sucked at Shantih's plunging hooves. Jinny's hands were knotted into her mane. The metal sky pressing down above them flamed scarlet as the Red Horse reared above the horizon. It stood, legs braced, crested neck arched, its head turning and turning as it searched the marsh with its flaming eyes. Shantih's struggles grew weaker. She no longer had the strength to try to escape. Jinny crouched close to her neck, shielding her face as the glare of its eyes beamed straight at her. The terrible whinnying of the Horse grew louder, more brazen. Jinny drowned in it.

She sat up. Heard the whinnying coming from the garden and sprang across to the window. To her dismay, she saw that Shantih had broken out of her field and was raking about the garden, crashing her way through shrubberies, rhododendron thickets and flower beds. Jinny grabbed her anorak from the back of a chair and, thinking only of what Ken would say if Shantih got into his vegetable garden, raced downstairs.

I'll need a halter, Jinny thought, knowing that when Shantih was excited she had no hope of holding her by her forelock.

Jinny unlocked the kitchen door, tore down the path to the stables. Somewhere in Finmory's grounds she could hear Shantih plunging about, her strident whinnying shattering the moonlit silence.

The hook where the halters were meant to hang was empty. The last person to use them, probably herself, hadn't put them back in the right place. But Shantih's bridle was hanging from its hook. Jinny snatched it up and ran back into the garden.

'Shantih,' she called. 'Shantih.' She stood still to listen.

Jinny heard the sound of Shantih's hooves and ran towards it.

'Steady, the horse, steady,' she shouted. 'Come on then, Shantih.'

The sound of hooves stopped. The silent night breathed back. Jinny stood still, feeling the silence prickling on the nape of her neck.

Then Shantih whickered with the welcoming tremble of sound that Jinny knew so well. Plunging her way through the dark blotch of rhododendrons, Shantih came galloping straight at Jinny. For a panicked moment, Jinny thought she wasn't going to stop, then, within inches of where Jinny stood, the Arab skidded to a halt. Her mane was twined with creepers, spiky with rhododendron leaves, her nostrils and eyes wild with her galloping. She stretched out her neck and rested her head on Jinny's outstretched hand.

Jinny slipped the reins over Shantih's head, eased the bit into her mouth and settled the headpiece over her ears. Shantih waited with her head low, accepting the bridle, as Jinny buckled the throatlash.

For a moment Jinny paused, standing against Shantih's shoulder, the thought wordless in her mind that she would go for a ride, gallop Shantih over the moonlit hills.

Jinny leaped and landed easily astride Shantih. She felt the horse warm and solid, comfortingly real.

'Where to?' whispered Jinny, and saw Shantih's ears tickle with the sound of her voice, heard her nostrils flittering in answer. Jinny eased her fingers on the reins and Shantih broke into a trot. Without hesitating, Shantih took the track that led onto the moors. As they passed the black shape of Finmory House and climbed up over the rough, bracken-clad slopes, Shantih's trot changed into a steady canter.

At first Jinny tried to slow her down, tugging pointlessly at the reins. Then she remembered how Shantih had run with Mr MacKenzie's herd of Shetland ponies. Often on moonlit nights like this they must have galloped for the joy of it over the open moors.

Jinny relaxed, let her horse gallop on, let herself be carried to wherever Shantih wanted to take her. She gazed over the dark waves of moorland, at the bulk of mountains cramped down onto the brink of this moonlit world, and up into the huge immensity of the sky. She was only conscious of her horse, taken up and carried by this pounding urgency. A grey shape flowed at Shantih's heels. Jinny saw him, had no words to say 'Kelly', but was comforted by his being there.

As she rode, a voice sang in Jinny – a high, sweet singing.

Loch Varrich was a sheet of unbroken silver, mist wreathed over its surface. The gnarled pines that grew by its shore were etched, black claws against the bright sky.

When they reached the head of Loch Varrich, Shantih turned to the right. Without hesitation she took the path that led through the peat bog to Brachan.

Through the trance that held Jinny powerless, she tried to turn Shantih, but nothing she did had any effect on the relentless speed of her horse.

Have to go where she takes me, Jinny thought, each word thick in her mind as if her head was full of cotton wool. *Have no choice.*

Jinny had no knowledge of time. She clung helplessly to Shantih's mane. Tired now, she jolted and slipped, longing to fall and lie in the heather. But something of the will that drove Shantih on forced Jinny not to give in. Somehow it mattered that she should stay on Shantih, that she should survive.

Water from the peat bog spurted diamonds under Shantih's hooves. Her speed sprayed water over Jinny's head. As Shantih came to the deepest part of the bog she slowed to a trot, then plunged and reared her way through it.

Once clear of the bog, Shantih galloped on, showing no signs of tiredness. The mists grew denser. Sometimes they seemed to be riding through drifts of cloud, sometimes only Shantih's head and throat were visible, moving, disembodied, in front of Jinny, and at other times Shantih's hooves splashed through waves of mist.

Shantih began to canter downhill, and Jinny realised dimly that they must have reached Brachan. The mist was like an icy blanket, clinging to everything. Jewels of moisture glinted in Shantih's mane and Jinny's long hair. It was so cold. Jinny had stopped feeling anything. She was only vaguely aware of where she was, of who she was. Only the will remained, the force that came from somewhere outside of herself so that she could not give way, could not sink back into unconsciousness.

A wind blew aside the curtains of mist and, for a moment, Jinny saw the crofts of Brachan and the schoolhouse where the archaeologists were staying, then Shantih reared away from the buildings and began to gallop uphill. She stopped for a moment by the scarred hillside where the dig was in progress, then trotted away from it. She paused as if listening, then cantered on and stopped again. She stood with her head stretched forward into the sheeting, moving mists as if sensing something that Jinny could not see.

Jinny sat numbly on her back, waiting for her to canter on, but still Shantih stood without moving. At last Jinny slid to the ground. She tried to speak to her horse, but her lips were numb with cold and too clumsy for speech. She could do nothing but lean helplessly against Shantih. Kelly pushed at her knee, whining and clawing at her leg. Jinny lifted her face from Shantih's neck to look down at him.

'To have come all this way,' Jinny said to the dog. His amber eyes gazed back at her.

Shantih began to walk steadily forward. No longer searching for a way, each stride sure and positive. Jinny walked beside her, holding her reins loosely in her hand. She was no longer afraid. All her fears had gone. The certainty that filled her horse was with Jinny too. This was where she should be. It was right for her to be here.

Crossing the rough ground, Jinny's feet found their own way. She didn't stumble or trip but walked easily, as if she followed a path she knew as well as the path between Finmory and the stables.

Jinny had no idea how long she walked at Shantih's side. It could have been hours or minutes. There was only the present moment. The Horse moving with power and grace beside her. The pad of an animal loping at her heels.

The mists shimmered and flowed about them, then suddenly drifted apart, and Jinny saw that they had reached a hollow in the moor. It was completely circular, as if someone had dug it out of the hillside; a smooth cup with steep rocky sides. There was only one way into it – the path which Shantih was following.

At first, it seemed to Jinny that the ground was mounded with heaps of skins, then one moved, and

Jinny knew they were human. They crouched close to the hillside, their long, matted hair and skin clothing making them look as if they were part of the earth, still rooted in it. Jinny smelled again the fetid, rancid stench she had smelled when she rode with the Pony Folk.

They had left a pathway between them to the far side of the clearing. Shantih followed it without hesitation. She looked straight ahead, her neck arched proudly under its garlands of white flowers and leaves.

At the far side of the clearing was a woman wearing long robes. Her white hair fell about her like a waterfall. Her face was brown-skinned and furrowed with deep wrinkles. Her eyes were a pale, washed blue. Behind her was a high block of stone. A fire was burning in front of the stone, and, as Shantih approached, the woman threw handfuls of dried leaves and flowers onto the flames. They flared up, blue green, and a heavy, sweet smell spread from the fire.

Jinny's hand held the rope of twisted creepers. The robes she was wearing made her movements stiff and slow. As she stood in front of the altar, her lips moved in a droning chant.

Two small statues were on the altar, one on either side of a golden bowl. One was Epona. The other, about the same size, was of a Horse. It's simple shape was made out of metal. The head was an Arab's head, the tail kinked over its quarters was an Arab's tail.

The old woman's hand moved again, sprinkling

148

more herbs into the flames. The two statues grew huge. The Pony Folk moaned with a low terror. Jinny flung herself onto the ground, pressing her face into the earth to block out the fearful thing that towered above her. The Horse on the altar was the Red Horse, rearing above them all, while Epona, an apple in her outstretched hand, watched and waited.

'No!' cried Jinny. 'No!'

When she lifted her head the mists had rolled back, blotting out all traces of the Pony Folk. Jinny stood up, still shaking, Shantih's reins clutched tightly in her hand. There was nothing to be seen but white, billowing mists.

Jinny climbed stiffly back onto Shantih. When her horse moved forward, Jinny almost fell. She twisted her reins round her hands and dug her fingers into Shantih's mane as they cantered through the mists.

The ride back to Finmory seemed to be happening to someone else, not to Jinny. As if she were in a safe place, watching another skinny, red-headed girl clinging to the back of a galloping horse; watching the horse plunging through the bog, the girl spreadeagled, her arms round the horse's neck; watching them by the shores of Loch Varrich, silhouetted against the silver water, and, at last, galloping over the moors to Finmory.

When Jinny slipped to the ground by Shantih's field she was trembling with exhaustion. It took her minutes to undo Shantih's throatlash. Her useless fingers wouldn't grasp the leather. By the time she had taken the bridle off and watched Shantih walk off into the field, tears were running down Jinny's face, her whole body shaking.

As she shut the gate, Jinny remembered that Shantih had escaped from the field. Maybe she had broken through the hedge and would get out again. But Jinny was too tired to check. Surely after her night galloping, Shantih would stay where she was. She had joined Pippen and was grazing by his side. Even if she had been tearing round the field Jinny could have done nothing about it. She had to sleep.

Left foot, right foot, Jinny made her slow deliberate way to the stable and hung up Shantih's bridle. Right foot, left foot, she moved like a robot along the path, through the back door into the kitchen and up to her bedroom. She collapsed on her bed. Her eyes shut. Clearly, before she gave way to sleep, she saw the stone altar. The Horse alone on it, for Epona was locked in the case in the Wilton Collection.

Where is the Horse now? she wondered, and sat up, as if there was something she must do about it, that only she could do. Then she slumped back across the bed. 'Tomorrow,' she mumbled. 'Tomorrow.' And was asleep.

$\mathcal{T}en$

'Jinny! Jinny! Are you awake?' called Sue's voice from the foot of Jinny's stairs. 'Come on. Get up. It's a smashing morning.'

Jinny woke. For a moment she couldn't think who was calling her. Then she realised to her amazement that she was wearing her anorak and muddy shoes.

'Come on,' called Sue again. 'Get up.'

'Right. I'm up,' Jinny called back, thinking, *Of course, it's Sue. She stayed for the night because they're all away.*

'I'll start and make breakfast,' Sue shouted, and Jinny heard her footsteps going back down to the kitchen.

Jinny sat on the edge of her bed. She couldn't think why she was still dressed. Then slowly the night's happenings came back to her. Piece by piece, like a jigsaw, they fitted together in her mind. The night ride, the mists, the Pony Folk, the woman with the white cascade of hair, the altar with the two statues on it. One had been Epona, the same statuette as Jinny had lifted out of the case in the Wilton Museum. The other of an Arab horse. Jinny sat staring into space. Thinking about it, she felt as if she was falling backwards, slipping, falling.

She jumped off her bed.

It must have been a dream, she thought. *I must have dreamed it. I must have heard Shantih in the garden before I undressed, gone down and caught her, come back here and fallen asleep at once. I couldn't have ridden to Brachan. I couldn't have seen the Pony Folk. They're all dead, hundreds and hundreds of years ago. Time is solid. You can't swim about in it. It must have been a dream.*

Jinny checked through the window to make sure that Shantih was in her field with Pippen, then she hurried downstairs.

'Where are you going?' Sue demanded, as Jinny hurried through the kitchen.

'Just out for a minute,' Jinny called back. 'Just checking.'

She hurried down to the stables. Shantih's bridle was hanging from its hook. Jinny took it down and inspected it. There was dried grass on the snaffle, but that could easily have been from yesterday afternoon.

There was nothing about the bridle to tell her whether it had been used last night or not.

If I did ride Shantih through the bog again, her legs will be muddy and peaty, Jinny thought suddenly. *That will prove whether it was real or not.*

When Jinny reached the field, Shantih was standing by the burn, drinking. She stopped when she saw Jinny, and came to meet her, splashing through the mud at the edges of the burn. Her sides were plastered with wet mud where she had been rolling. Even if there had been dried peat on Shantih, Jinny couldn't have seen it now.

But it must have been a dream, Jinny told herself as she walked back to the kitchen. *It couldn't have been anything else.* Jinny had taken a short cut up to the house through the dense shrubbery that was still hopelessly overgrown. A branch clung to Jinny's sleeve. She plucked it loose by its leaves. A sweet pungent smell filled her nostrils and, for a second, the Horse reared in terrifying power before her.

'You want to do what?' demanded Sue in astonishment.

'Ride over to the dig,' repeated Jinny. She hadn't told Sue anything about her dream, if it had been a dream. 'I just want to see it again.'

'But you said you never wanted to go back, never wanted to see any of them again. And you were so rude to them.'

'You can be sure,' said Jinny, eating the egg Sue had boiled for her, 'that when you hear me say I'm never going to do a thing again, that's the very next thing I'll be doing. Things change.'

'Your family will wonder what's happened to you if they get back and you're not here.'

'We'll leave them a note,' said Jinny. 'But if we hurry we can be back before them. I don't suppose they'll be home before the evening.'

'Say your father phones?'

'He'll only think I'm out with Shantih. He won't worry.'

'What do you want to go back for?'

'I've told you. I just do. You don't need to come if you don't want to.'

'I'll come,' agreed Sue. 'Perhaps it will take a few more ounces off Pippen. We're not going over the hills though, are we?'

Jinny hesitated. Last night Shantih had gone through the bog as if it was hardly there. She had hardly noticed it. But that had been a dream. This morning the bog would be real.

'No,' Jinny said. 'We'll go round by the road.'

Their horses trotted out well, hooves clipping the tarmac, ears pricked, going steadily forward.

'Of course,' Sue was saying, 'you can't expect cavalletti to make any difference if you don't work at it. You must school every day.'

'Not much chance of that if they make me send her to Miss Tuke's.'

Sue's conversation rippled the surface of Jinny's mind. She answered Sue, hardly hearing what she was saying, just making the right noises to keep Sue chatting. Underneath, she was thinking of what she would do when they reached the dig. She knew that where the archaeologists were excavating was not the right place where the stone altar had been last night. Jinny wanted to see if she could find it again – the rounded hollow with its high stone sides and its straight path leading to the altar.

'Maybe Miss Tuke would school her over cavalletti for you?' suggested Sue.

'Shouldn't think Miss Tuke would even know what cavalletti are,' said Jinny.

When they reached Brachan, they stopped at the schoolhouse. Sue held Shantih while Jinny knocked on the door.

'No one in,' Jinny said, coming back to Sue. 'They must all be up at the dig. Shall we put them in the field or ride up?'

'Better leave them in the field. Now we're here, I expect we'll need to help for a bit, and I shouldn't think Shantih would fancy walking to and fro while you carry buckets.'

'Right there,' said Jinny, and they led their horses down to the field and took off their tack.

'Will she stay?' Sue asked, looking back anxiously at Shantih, who was trotting back and forward along the hedge and pushing at the gate. 'She does fuss, doesn't she?'

'Perhaps if you could see what she can see you'd be making a fuss too. All depends how it is for each person. No one else can tell what it's like for someone else.'

'Well, Pippen is in exactly the same field and he's settled down.'

'That's what I'm saying,' said Jinny. 'The way Pippen sees the field tells him its OK, safe to go on stuffing himself, but the way Shantih sees it tells her it isn't.' Jinny dumped her tack in the porch of the schoolhouse. 'I'll come down and see that she's all right at lunchtime.'

'Well,' said Freda, when they arrived at the dig, 'nice to see you again. Come to give us a hand?'

'For a bit,' said Jinny. 'We wanted to go for a long ride so we thought we'd come here.'

'Glad you did. Go and see Jerry. He'll be grateful for a bit of help.'

Jerry was pink and specky. He was labouring to fill in one of the pits they had excavated.

'Very important to leave the site as you found it,' he told them without much conviction. He pointed out a pile of rubble. 'That's to go back in as well,' he said, finding them a bucket each.

Jinny trudged back and forward, obediently filling her bucket, carrying it to the hole and tipping it in. Now that she was back at Brachan, the memory of her dream was vivid in her mind. She searched the hillside, trying to pick out any spot that looked as if it might have been the hollowed bowl where they had worshipped Epona and the Horse.

But it isn't anywhere real, Jinny thought, trying to convince herself. *It was a place in a dream. I can't possibly find it here.*

'Station break. Everybody out,' yelled one of the students.

'Gosh,' said Jerry, 'am I glad of that. Say, what about you two? Wonder if there'll be enough grub.'

'We brought our own sandwiches,' Sue told him as they walked across to where everyone was settling down on the grass for lunch.

'I'm going back down to the schoolhouse to see if my horse is OK,' Jinny announced in a general sort of way.

'What a shame,' said one girl. 'You should have gone before it was lunchtime.'

'Do you want me to come?' asked Sue.

'Oh no,' said Jinny quickly. 'I'll not be long. If she is still messing about I might give her a gallop to calm her down,' she added, in case Sue might see her riding over the moor and think she had been deserted.

Jinny ran lightly over the hillside, picked up Shantih's

bridle, and ran on down to the field where Shantih was waiting by the gate.

Jinny rode up the moors, keeping far enough away from the dig so that no one could call to ask where she was going. Sitting high on Shantih, looking down on the archaeologists, Jinny remembered how she had seen them as sheep, not knowing what they were doing, and she remembered the expressions on the faces of the Pony Folk, their wistful longing, their hopelessness. The way they had turned to look at her as if they were depending on her to help them. A choking, heady excitement flowed through Jinny as she felt Shantih's stride quicken and become more definite.

As she rode, Jinny searched the hillside for any hollow which might once have held the altar to Epona and the Horse.

It could be anywhere, she thought hopelessly. *It was so long ago. Probably the hollow is all filled in by now. I'll never find it. It was only a dream. You don't find dream places on a real moor.* Jinny almost turned Shantih back down to the dig. But under all her common-sense doubts there was a certainty, a knowing that was more sure than anything else, that made her go on searching.

Probably I wouldn't even know the place if I rode over it, Jinny thought, but she went on walking Shantih about the moor, all the time staring about her. With each change of perspective, Jinny searched for traces of the straight way that had led them over the moors and taken her through the Pony Folk to stand in front of the altar.

Suddenly Shantih stopped, her whole being electric and tense. She gave a shrill whicker and, without any hesitation, began to trot out as if she was following an invisible path over the moor.

Shantih went on, straight ahead, flirting her nostrils, knowing where she was going, but still Jinny could see nothing ahead that bore any resemblance to her dream hollow. Shantih was pushing her way through the red-gold, rusty fronds of bracken. As they went on, the bracken seemed to grow higher and more dense, it's fronds parting like a bow wave as Shantih made her way through it. Jinny glanced back and saw that they had left no track through the red-gold sea. It had closed behind them, covering over all traces of their passage.

Shantih stopped. She stood perfectly still. Jinny closed her legs against her sides but Shantih refused to move. Impatiently, Jinny kicked her on. There was no sign here of the hollow in the hills, only the waves of bracken. Yet still Shantih refused to go forward. Jinny jumped to the ground, took her reins over her head and led her forward. The bracken was so deep that it reached Jinny's shoulders.

Normally, when Jinny had walked through bracken, the ground was rough and treacherous under her feet, but here she seemed to be able to walk as surely as if she were on the open hillside, and Shantih moved freely at her side.

Jinny stopped at the same moment as Shantih. She laid the palm of her hand on the chestnut's neck and looked about her. They were standing in a hollow in the bracken. It was as if the land here had been scooped out, but no one would ever have been able to detect it unless they had come the way Jinny had come and stood where she was standing now.

Jinny shivered. Her skin prickled with a sudden charge. For the blink of an eye she saw the hollow as it had been when the Pony Folk had worshipped here, when the old woman had sprinkled her herbs on the flames, drugging their minds and making Epona and the Horse change into gods before their worshippers' eyes.

Hardly knowing what she was doing, Jinny knelt in the bracken. Its fronds closed her into a rust-red world. Blind, she stretched out her hands in front of her and dug into the mould with her fingers. Frantically she dredged the humus through her fingers, feeling bracken roots and stones, and the gentle texture of decay. Her left hand closed on smooth metal; fingered it clean from the mould.

Jinny stood up, and on the palm of her hand lay the small statue of the Horse. The craftsman or priest who had made it so many centuries ago had known that it was an Arab. There on Jinny's hand was the goggle eye, the wide nostril and the curved Arab face, the tail kinked high over the little statue's quarters.

Jinny stared at it. Shantih stretched out her neck and breathed gently over the statue. Moors and sky slipped away. There was only herself, Shantih, and this most precious thing, taken out of the darkness and standing now, on her hand.

Jinny's hand closed over it. She held it tight. The moors and sky were back – real, enclosing – bringing with them the thought of Sue, who would want to know what Jinny had been doing, and the archaeologists, who would have to be told about her find; who would want to take it away from her.

Jinny shut her hand round the Horse, clutching it tightly.

I found it, she thought. *They shan't have it.*

Quickly Jinny looked over her shoulder, afraid that someone might have seen her find it, then laughed at herself – for who could possibly have been watching her on the empty moors?

For minutes longer she stood rubbing the metal with her finger, awed by the strangeness of her find. If last night had been a dream, then it had been a true dream. Yet how could it have been a dream when Shantih had known her way to where the altar had once stood?

With great care, Jinny wrapped the Horse in her handkerchief, then put it back into her anorak pocket and rode back to the schoolhouse.

If I tell them about it they won't let me take it back to Finmory, Jinny thought as she rode. *They'll say it's too valuable, and take it away from me at once. But it was me who found it. I'm not meant to give it to them.*

When she had returned Shantih to Pippen and the field, Jinny took the bridle back to the porch. Hidden in the doorway, Jinny took the Horse out of her pocket and unwrapped the handkerchief just enough to let herself see it again.

She could, if she chose to, run up to the dig and tell them all how she had found the Horse. They would praise her, ask her questions, each person wishing that they had found it instead of Jinny. When they locked it away in a museum they would put a label by it saying that it had been found by Jennifer Manders.

For a moment Jinny hesitated. She would like all those things, would enjoy being the centre of attention. If she told the archaeologists, she would be able to tell her family. When Petra came back from Glasgow, full of her undoubted success, Jinny would be able to tell her about the statue she had found. When Ken came back she could tell him about her dream and how Shantih had led her to where the bracken grew over the Celtic altar.

If she told the archaeologists. But Jinny was sure that she wasn't meant to do that.

Jinny started violently, sprang round, thinking she had heard someone move behind her. There was no one. Fumbling in her haste, Jinny wrapped the statue back in her handkerchief and put it in the bag with her uneaten sandwiches. She tied the bag back onto Shantih's saddle.

'You've been ages,' Sue exclaimed when Jinny got back to the dig. 'I was beginning to think that you'd gone home without me.'

'I didn't mean to go so far,' Jinny said. 'Sorry.'

'Come and do a bit more bucketing and then I think we'd better get back.'

'OK,' said Jinny, gladly setting to work again, not looking at anyone.

She worked twice as hard as she had done in the morning, hurrying between the pile of earth and the pit, which didn't seem to fill up at all, no matter how much earth was tipped back into it.

'Nearly three o'clock,' said Sue, making Jinny start with fright. 'You are jittery. Nearly as bad as Shantih.'

'I didn't realise you were there,' said Jinny lamely.

'Well, I have been here all day,' said Sue. 'But maybe you hadn't noticed. I was only saying that I thought it was time to go home.'

They went to say goodbye to Freda.

'Nice to have seen you again,' she said. 'Only sorry we haven't been able to unearth a Horse god for you. Still, next year we're going to try over there.' and Freda pointed to where Jinny had found the statue. 'Their holy places often lay to the East of their settlements.'

Jinny felt her face reddening. She stared down at her feet. *I'm not telling them*, she thought. And she held her tongue between her teeth to stop herself blurting out the story of her find.

Several times on the way home Jinny nearly told Sue, but each time the thought of Sue insisting that they return the Horse to the archaeologists stopped her.

I will tell her, Jinny thought. *I will tell her sometime.*

'I'd better take Pippen back to his field,' said Sue, when they reached Finmory. 'Then I think I should drop in and see Mum. Will your father be back?'

'They'll probably all be back,' said Jinny. 'And if they're not, they will be soon.'

'See you tomorrow, then,' and Sue rode off.

There was no car outside Finmory. Mr Manders wasn't back. Jinny hurried Shantih through her feed and turned her out. In the tack room she opened her sandwich bag and took out her handkerchief with the Horse inside it. She was desperate to see the statue again, but she didn't look at it in the tack room. Holding it carefully in her hand, she carried it into the house and up to her bedroom.

Eleven

Kneeling on the floor in front of her mural, Jinny unwrapped the statue. There was no possible doubt, it was the same one that Jinny had seen on the altar next to Epona. And it was an Arab. The dished face carried with an Arab's pride and arrogance was so completely different to the head and neck of the pony Epona was seated on. It couldn't have been chance. Epona was riding a native pony, while the Horse was an Arab.

Jinny set the Horse down in front of the mural. She went back to the opposite wall and sat down cross-legged on the floor, trying to see both the Red Horse of the mural and the Celtic Horse god. Kelly came padding upstairs, pushed open Jinny's door and lay down beside her, his forelegs outstretched, his nose placed exactly between his paws, his eyes gazing through grey thatch at the Horse.

B.C., thought Jinny. *It was made and worshipped before Christ was born.* All the history she had been taught at school, the billion, trillion, zillions of people, all the mixed-up stories in Jinny's head of King Alfred's cakes, the Princes in the Tower, Henry V and Walter Raleigh, had all happened, if they had happened at all, while the little metal horse had lain in the ground above Brachan.

Waiting for me to find it, thought Jinny. *They wanted me to find it, not those sheep-brained archaeologists.*

Just for a second she remembered how the Horse had appeared when the old woman had sprinkled her herbs on the flames; just for a second the Red Horse reared into Jinny's mind, searching, questing the air for the lost thing it had come to find.

Jinny shuddered with terror. She didn't know what to do. She held the little Horse tightly in her hand, feeling it real and solid. She had found it, but she didn't know what to do next. Only knew that she would never give it to the archaeologists. *They would take it away and it belongs here*, she thought.

Jinny heard the sound of their car stopping in front of the house and car doors being opened. She wrapped the statue back in her handkerchief, brought her cash box down from the top of her wardrobe, dragged off its swaddlings of Sellotape and thrust the horse into it.

'Jinny, Jinny, are you in?' called her mother, as Jinny put the cash box back, jumped down from the chair

166

and ran downstairs to see her family.

'How did it go?' she asked Petra. 'Bet you were brilliant. A distinction. Bet you did.'

'I don't actually know,' said Petra. 'They don't actually say, but I could tell they were pleased with me.'

'Oh, super, super,' enthused Jinny. 'And are they going to film your book?' she asked, turning to her father. 'Did they think it was the utter, utter best they've ever read?'

'They're certainly going to publish it,' said Mr Manders, 'and things are looking good for the TV link-up.'

'Great,' said Jinny. 'That is fantastic.'

'Were you all right by yourself?' asked her father.

''Course I was. Sue came up. We had a super time. Of course I was all right. We built a triple and I jumped Shantih over it and Sue's showing me how to ride over cavalletti.'

Words frothed out of Jinny. She was so glad to see her family again, she could hardly stand still. No matter how exciting a time her father had had in London, no matter how successful Petra had been, it was nothing compared to Jinny's secret.

'You seem to have enjoyed yourself,' said Mrs Manders, looking at her flushed, excited daughter. 'You're all catherine wheels.'

'Expect it's jumping that horse,' said Petra.

'Oh yes,' agreed Jinny. 'She flies over the jumps – higher and higher. There is nothing Shantih couldn't jump if she wanted to.'

That night, Jinny waited until all her family had settled down to sleep before she unwrapped the Horse statue. She didn't want to risk any of them coming into the room and seeing it.

Jinny sat on the floor, holding the statue. *From so long ago*, she thought. *Who made you? What are you? And now I've found you, you'll always stay here.* Jinny clutched the Horse tightly in her hand.

The house settled into silence. The Red Horse glowed out of the wall. The yellow circles of its eyes glared down at Jinny. Lost in wonder at the Horse she was holding, Jinny had forgotten her fears. Now they came flooding back. The waiting presence of the Red Horse was still there. She jumped up, shaking the fear out of her head.

No, she told herself. *Now I've found the Horse I don't need to be afraid any longer. I've done what the dreams wanted me to do.*

Jinny lifted her hand to strike the mural, to reassure herself that it was only a painting, but she couldn't bring her hand down to slap it. She stood frozen with her hand upraised, then spun round, away from the mural and ran through to the other half of her room.

She got undressed and into her nightdress. Stood daring herself to go back and look at the mural, but her nerve broke and she sprang into bed, pulling the bedclothes over her head, the Horse still clutched tightly in her hand.

Outside, the night stillness was broken by a sudden tempest of hooves. It could only be Shantih galloping round her field. Yet it seemed to Jinny that the hoofbeats gusted over the roof, circled over the moors and waited there.

Jinny lay, tight and shivering, her knees tucked to her chin, straining to hear. Afraid that she would hear the hooves again, yet more afraid that she wouldn't hear them and the Red Horse would take her by surprise. Suddenly she was too tired to care. The need for sleep was a lead weight inside her head. In a moment of total terror, Jinny knew that she must sleep, and that in her sleep the Red Horse was still waiting for her.

Shantih was deep in the mire, already tiring, too weak to struggle much longer. The heat from the flaming sky burnt Jinny's lungs with every breath she drew. On the horizon the Red Horse reared. It swung its head to and fro, the beams from its yellow eyes searching over the black water of the bog. Then it focused on Jinny where she clung desperately to Shantih. Before, the Red Horse had been a mindless force of destruction, but now its will was sharpened and directed. It had found what it was looking for. It was looking for the statue that Jinny was clutching in her hand. With nightmare hooves, the Horse came galloping at Jinny. Clouds of steam rose around it until there was only the noise of its hooves and the glare of its eyes as it galloped towards her.

'Jinny, Jinny, wake up. You're dreaming. Wake up.'

Her father's hand gripped her shoulder through the bedclothes, shaking her awake.

Jinny's head surfaced from under the blankets. She was drenched with sweat. For seconds she still struggled to escape, not knowing where she was.

'By goodness, that was some nightmare,' said her father. 'I thought I'd never get you out of it.'

Jinny pushed her hair back from her face and sat up, taking care to keep the statue hidden. She couldn't stop shivering. The Red Horse had been so close.

'Whatever were you dreaming about?'

'I can't remember,' lied Jinny. 'I can only remember screaming.'

'You were certainly doing that. Can I get anything for you?'

'No,' said Jinny. 'I might go down and make myself a mug of chocolate.'

'Good idea,' said her father. 'Wake yourself up properly. You don't want to fall back into that.'

When her father had gone, Jinny wrapped the statue up again and put it back in her cash box. She got dressed and went downstairs, where she found her favourite pony book about two girls in a Shropshire village who ran a riding school during their summer holidays. Jinny took it into the kitchen, stirred up the Aga, made herself chocolate to drink and a tomato sandwich to eat, then she sat down to read.

She knew the book as well as she knew the story of the three bears – bringing the ponies into the stables in the morning, trotting them bareback through the summer lanes; the grey pony borrowed from the milkman who won the local showjumping class, the thoroughbred given to them by Major Grant because he couldn't control it, and Midget the almost carthorse. Sitting crouched over the Aga, reading, the security of the story, wove a warm web round Jinny. No danger. No dreams. Only summer days filled with riding school ponies. They held back the terror of the Red Horse.

'Have you been up all night?' Jinny's mother asked, surprised to find Jinny setting the table for breakfast.

'Well, I had a bad dream,' said Jinny, not committing herself.

'You certainly had. What is worrying you? Can't you tell me? How can I help you if you won't tell me what's wrong?'

'I don't know how you even need to ask,' said Jinny. 'There's so many things for me to worry about that I have to make a list to remind myself of them all.'

'You were bursting out all over when we came home last night. What was that about?'

'I told you – Shantih jumping so well. She could

171

jump the sun,' cried Jinny, flinging her arm in a wide, sun-clearing arc.

Mrs Manders, realising that she was getting nowhere, stopped asking questions.

Jinny spent the day helping her father in the pottery. Sue came over to see if she wanted to ride.

'Thought you'd want to school,' said Sue. 'Trotting Shantih over cavaletti once isn't going to do her any good. You have to do it every day, go on teaching her.'

'I'm giving her a rest day,' stated Jinny.

'From what we've heard,' said Mr Manders, 'Shantih is ready for the high jump at Wembley after the way she was jumping yesterday.'

'Yesterday?' said Sue. 'We didn't . . .'

Jinny dropped the sugar basin she was decorating. She didn't want her father to find out about their return visit to Brachan.

'Idiot child!' exclaimed Mr Manders. 'That was part of a set.'

Jinny picked up the pieces, and Sue said if she wasn't riding that was that, and umbraged out of the pottery.

Jinny settled down. In the bright morning pottery, safe with her father beside her, Jinny could relax. With sure strokes she painted pots. Ken said it was dishonest to decorate other people's pots, but he wasn't there to make her feel guilty. Ken wouldn't be back until tomorrow.

At intervals throughout the day, Jinny escaped to

her bedroom, took the statue out of her cash box and sat on the edge of her bed, holding it, looking at it, then quickly hiding it away again.

After tea, Jinny went down to see Shantih. She leaned over the field gate watching her horse graze. The fields reaching down to the bay, the glimmer of sea and the jet jaws of the cliffs swam hazily in front of Jinny's eyes. She knew them so well, on so many evenings Jinny had stood where she was standing now, being content.

The air from the sea seemed suddenly less clear, as if a mist had blown in from the water. Jinny blinked her eyes, but the dense air massed and grew thicker. It towered in over the fields, rising in swirling clouds from the ground to the sky.

Jinny stared, mesmerised. Through the mist came the crash of waves breaking on the shore, the thunder of hooves. Jinny caught a glimpse of the Red Horse, monstrous through the mists, its yellow eyes glared straight at her. She screamed aloud, ran flat out, feet slapping, hair flying out behind her, as she bolted for home.

'Now what's wrong?' exclaimed her mother in exasperation, as Jinny slammed the kitchen door behind her and leaned against it, gasping for breath. 'You look as if you'd seen a ghost.'

'I thought I saw,' began Jinny, but she couldn't go on. The terror that gripped her was her own private terror. She had to find her own way through it. If she told anyone else they would only make her give the statue back to the archaeologists, and Jinny knew that she must not do that.

'Saw what?'

'Oh nothing.'

'Then fold these sheets with me,' said her mother, making the kitchen warm and safe.

And, for a moment, Jinny thought that all she had to do was to give the Horse to the archaeologists and all her life would be like this again. The fear that pursued her everywhere would leave her alone.

No, said the voice in Jinny. 'No.'

'Pardon?' said Mrs Manders.

'I was saying, "no",' replied Jinny. 'No to everything, because that's the way I feel.'

Jinny sat pretending to read, knowing that soon her parents would realise how late it was and insist that she went to bed. The thought of going to sleep, knowing that the Red Horse was waiting for her, choked in Jinny's throat. Perhaps she would ask Petra if she could put the camp bed up in her room and sleep there.

Shocked at herself for even thinking such a thing, Jinny pushed the temptation to the back of her mind. Petra would never forget it. She would always remember.

'That is eleven o'clock!' cried Mrs Manders. 'And you're still sitting here, Jinny. Go on, off with you.'

At the door, Jinny paused. *Don't ask*, she told herself. *Don't ask*. Then she turned back and heard herself say to Petra, 'Could I come and sleep in your room. Could I put the camp bed up? Please.'

Jinny saw Petra and her mother look quickly at each other.

'Of course you can,' said her mother. 'I wanted to suggest it to you, but you know what you're like.'

'I don't mind a bit,' said Petra.

Jinny wanted to run and hug them. They had saved her from the Red Horse. Perhaps she would never need to go back to her own room, could always share with Petra.

'I'll help you put the camp bed up,' offered Petra, and bustled Jinny out of the room.

'Really, you can stop being so silly,' Petra was saying, her voice reaching Jinny through the darkness to where she lay stiffly on the narrow camp bed. 'You'll enjoy living in the hostel. You won't actually have a room of your own until you're into third year. In first year there's three of you to one room, but the partitions make it almost as good as your own room. They don't mind a bit what posters you put up on your own bit of wall.'

Even in the dark, Jinny could sense the tidiness of her sister's bedroom. The clothes she had taken off were hung up in the wardrobe, put away in drawers, or dropped into her pink plastic laundry basket.

'Of course, you have to be in by eight o'clock or get a late pass. Matron is pretty generous as long as you keep on the right side of her.'

'Can you hear anything?' demanded Jinny urgently. Behind the irritation of Petra's chatter, Jinny was sure she could hear the beat of hooves. Or was it her own breathing?

'Your bedsprings twanging,' said Petra. 'You'll find the beds in the hostel are very comfortable.'

The sound of the hooves came closer.

'Can't you hear the galloping?' Jinny cried desperately.

'What galloping? There's no galloping.'

But Jinny could hear it. Her hand under her pillow tightened on the statue.

'Goodnight,' said Petra. 'Don't have any of your nightmares in my room.'

Petra's breathing was controlled and even. She was asleep almost at once.

Jinny lay, tight under the darkness. The air about her reverberated with the thunder of hooves. The Red Horse was searching for its own. Jinny knew that she must sleep. The hoofbeats took away her will to stay awake. She could not think how she had been so foolish as to imagine that Petra's pink and white, sugar icing bedroom, her fashion magazines, her framed music diplomas, could ever hold back the force of the Red Horse.

Twelve

Ken came home the next afternoon.

'Tremendous,' he said. 'I start in Amsterdam in the middle of September.'

From the minute that Ken had received the letter, Jinny had been certain that he would go. *And maybe once he's with Bob Schultz, he'll meet other people, more like himself, and stay there. We'll hardly ever see him. He'll forget all about us*, she thought.

Jinny sat, lost in her own miseries, while Mr Manders told Ken about his visit to London and listened to details of Ken's arrangements to go to Amsterdam.

Despite her retreat to Petra's bedroom, Jinny's nightmare had been as vivid as ever, and now she was heavy with disgust at herself for being such a coward. Tonight she would sleep in her own room. It was true, you couldn't escape from things by running away from them.

'Did Kelly keep an eye on you?' Ken asked.

Jinny started back to her present surroundings and realised that there was only Ken and herself left in the room.

'Yes,' she said in surprise. 'How did you know?'

'Mentioned to him that you might need him.'

'Oh,' said Jinny, 'did you?'

Ken stood up, stretching up on his toes, his arms above his head, spreading out his fingers.

'How's Shantih?' he asked.

'Fine,' said Jinny, her voice polite and distant.

'Let's go and speak to her,' said Ken, and with long, light steps he was across the room and holding the door open for Jinny.

Jinny hesitated. She nearly made an excuse not to go with Ken, for she knew that part of her wanted to tell him about her find; wanted to show him the statue. Ken had always known that the Red Horse on Jinny's wall was magic. The very first time he had seen it he had known that there was a strangeness about it.

It was only fair that Ken should share the statue, but Jinny was afraid to tell him. She didn't think that Ken would want to tell the archaeologists, but she couldn't be sure. And somehow she felt that she couldn't ask anyone else what to do. She had to find out for herself.

'Coming?' Jinny realised that Ken was waiting for her.

'Oh, er, yes,' Jinny said, going out with him. 'But I can't be long. I've to, er, well, I've to be . . .'

'You can't be long,' interpreted Ken.

Jinny said nothing and they walked together down to Shantih's field.

'What's twisting you up?' asked Ken.

For a second, Jinny almost told him about her nightmares, her night ride back through time, the finding of the Horse and the continuing terror of her dreams. She so longed to be able to tell Ken that she had to bite her nails hard into the palms of her hands to stop the jangle of fear from bursting out of her.

'You look desperate,' said Ken, as they walked across the field to Shantih.

'Of course I'm desperate,' cried Jinny, barricading Ken out with words. 'I'm worried crazy about Shantih. You all think she's going to Miss Tuke's. You think it doesn't matter – that once I start school I'll forget all about her. Huh! Forget that someone else is feeding my horse; that someone else is riding her. Miss Tuke isn't good enough for Shantih. She can't ride. Will not ride Shantih. You all think it will be OK if I see Shantih at weekends and have her back for ten days at Christmas. You all think that's fine. Well it's not. And it's not going to happen. I'll find some way of stopping Miss Tuke from stealing my horse. That's what it is. It's stealing.'

Ken absorbed Jinny's aggression into his own silence. He ran his bony hand down Shantih's sleek neck, accepted her lipping caresses.

'Meeting Bob Schultz was like meeting someone I had known all my life,' he said. 'In the black days in Stopton I was so down that I couldn't even have hoped for a Bob Schultz. Couldn't even have wished for it to happen. It was all so black. But it has happened. I had to go through Stopton to meet Bob. "Joy and woe are woven fine." Be OK. You'll see.'

Jinny turned away quickly. 'I've got to get back,' she said, knowing that if she stayed another second she would tell Ken all that had happened.

That night, Jinny went back to her own room.

'I'm perfectly all right now,' she assured her family.

'You screamed last night,' said Petra. 'It took me ages to wake you up.'

'Then I wouldn't want to disturb you again,' said Jinny, ungrateful because the cowardly part of her wanted to stay with Petra. But she wasn't going to give into it a second time. 'I'm quite OK now,' she repeated.

Jinny didn't undress. She sat on top of her bed, her quilt wrapped round her shoulders, but, in spite of all she tried to do to stay awake, her eyes closed. She slept, and her dream came raging out of the shadows of her mind.

The Red Horse burned over the marsh, its yellow eyes beamed straight at Jinny where she lay over

Shantih's neck. One of Jinny's hands was knotted into Shantih's mane, but tonight her other hand clutched the statue of the Horse. The Red Horse was closer than it had ever been before.

Kelly woke her. He had pushed open her bedroom door, jumped up onto her bed and was clawing at her arm, licking her face and whimpering.

Jinny struggled free from her dream, sat blinking in the light, not knowing where she was. Then she cried, 'Kelly,' and clutched the dog to her, burying her face in his warm, shaggy coat. Normally Kelly never left Ken, and Jinny knew that Ken must have sent his dog to wake her.

Jinny reached her hand under her pillow and brought out the statue. She showed it to Kelly. The little Horse seemed more precious than ever. That she, Jinny Manders, should have been chosen to find such a hidden thing . . .

Never, thought Jinny. *I'll never, ever, give it to them.*

Kelly heard the hooves as well as Jinny. He sat suddenly alert, ears lifted, muzzle searching. The violent drumbeat of the hooves came down from the hills, seemed to Jinny to circle the house.

It's not my imagination, she thought. *Kelly can hear them too.*

Kelly jumped down from the bed, and stood facing the other half of Jinny's room. His hackles rising, lips drawn back, he stalked stiff-legged towards the archway.

181

'Kelly, come back. Come back here.'

The dog ignored her. A snarl rose in his throat as he paced on.

Jinny sprang off her bed, the statue still clutched in her hand. She made a grab at Kelly's collar, missed, grabbed again. As her hand gripped his collar, Jinny was through the archway. The Red Horse in her mural was burning, glowing, its yellow eyes starting from its head. The hooves outside became the beat of its hooves as it galloped free.

Jinny crouched in the corner of the room, powerless to run back to her bed, or to dash downstairs to Petra or her parents. She clutched Kelly to her as the room was filled with the presence of the Red Horse. It was the Horse of the mural, the Horse of Jinny's nightmares, the Horse that had been waiting for Jinny behind the standing stones, it was Shantih as she had been when she had run wild on the moors, as she was when Jinny saw her as a horse of the sun – and also it was the small, still, metal statue that Jinny clenched tightly in her hand.

Somehow Jinny struggled to her feet and, dragging Kelly with her, stumbled her way downstairs. She sat down at the table and buried her head in her arms. She couldn't go on like this. The terror of her nightmares was unbearable.

'Anything,' said Jinny aloud. 'I'll do anything if you'll only leave me alone.'

182

But Jinny didn't know what to do.

'You have been up all night again, haven't you?' asked her mother when she came down the next morning to find Jinny dozing in one of the kitchen chairs, Kelly at her feet. 'When did you last have a proper night's sleep?'

Jinny said nothing, because she wasn't sure herself.

'I'm having no more of this silliness,' said Mrs Manders. 'You look so ill. I'm phoning up Doctor Thornton and we're going to see him.'

'It wouldn't make any difference,' said Jinny bleakly. 'Not if I saw a hundred doctors, unless they could find a school for me at Finmory.'

'I don't think that is all that's disturbing you,' said her mother. 'There's something else that you won't tell us about.'

'Shall I help you with the breakfast?' asked Jinny, cutting off her mother.

After breakfast, Mrs Manders kept finding jobs for Jinny, and it was nearly eleven o'clock before she escaped to her bedroom. She stood at her window, staring out to the bay, trying desperately to think what she could do to escape from the Red Horse. *There must be some way*, she thought. *There must be. I can't give the statue to the archaeologists. I found it. It wasn't just chance. It's all connected with Shantih and my dream. I was meant to find it and now I've got to do something with it. I can't keep it here. I can't go on being afraid all the time. I've got to get rid of it somehow.*

And suddenly Jinny knew what she would do. She would find a secret place on the moors, a safe place where she could hide the statue, where it would never be disturbed again, where no archaeologists would come prowling and digging. It would be back in the earth, buried safely as it had been for so many hundreds of years.

'I'm going for a ride on the moors,' Jinny told her mother.

'With Sue?'

'No, by myself. It might be quite a long ride, so don't worry about me.'

'Don't do anything silly,' cautioned her mother, but Jinny had already gone.

Jinny urged Shantih on up the moor. The statue was safe in her anorak pocket.

It will need to be well out of sight of the house, Jinny thought. *Somewhere even Mr MacKenzie couldn't find it.* And that was the trouble, for where was there on the moor that would be safe from Mr MacKenzie's all-seeing eye? Jinny could just imagine him asking her what she had been doing, burying the wee horse on the moors when it should have been for the museum.

Then Jinny thought of the one place on the moor where Mr MacKenzie hardly ever visited – the old quarry. Forty years ago, the quarry had been closed.

Now its scarred sides were covered over with bracken, brambles, gorse and rowan trees, and if there hadn't been a barbed wire fence surrounding it, you would hardly have noticed it. It looked almost the same as the rest of the hillside. It would be the ideal place to hide the Horse. Jinny turned Shantih and began to ride towards it.

Jinny halted Shantih and stood looking down into the quarry. It was still possible to see the road that led down the side. Jinny could still make out the rusted metal rails where the trucks had run when they were working the quarry.

Looks OK to me, Jinny thought. *If I could get down to the bottom of it there would be lots of places where I could hide the Horse and no one would ever find it. In a way it's quite like the hollow at Brachan. A million times better than being shut in a dusty old museum.*

Once, the quarry had been wired off to stop anyone climbing down into it, but over the years the wire had grown brittle and rusted, the wooden posts had rotted away and no one had bothered to replace them. It would be easy now to get down into it.

Jinny looked round for a place where she could leave Shantih. There was nowhere at all. Jinny didn't want to risk tying her up by her reins. She would be too likely to pull back and break them.

The wire above the track down into the quarry was broken and decayed. *Shantih could easily step over that*, Jinny thought. *I could easily ride her down there. Then no one would see her. If I leave her tied up, Mr MacKenzie would be sure to see her and come over here noseying.*

Jinny rode Shantih to where the track sloped down into the overgrown depths of the quarry.

It looks perfectly safe to me, she thought.

There was nothing in Jinny's mind except her urgent need to bury the Horse again. No thought of Shantih's safety or her own. The many times she had been warned never to come near the quarry were completely forgotten. She had never been told not to ride into the quarry for no one had even thought of her doing such a crazy thing.

'Walk on, Shantih,' Jinny said, encouraging her horse to step over the broken, rusty strands of barbed wire.

Jinny rode between the rails, keeping to the middle of the track as it sloped steeply downwards. It was built on a high embankment, the sides of which were overgrown with a surging riot of bramble bushes, bracken and gorse, so that Jinny couldn't see the ground. She almost seemed to be riding along on top of the bushes.

Suddenly Shantih froze. There was something moving in the bushes just ahead.

'It's only a bird,' Jinny told her, knowing that it certainly wasn't a bird. 'It won't hurt you.' But Shantih wouldn't move.

The disturbance in the bushes came closer. Jinny couldn't see what it was. *Maybe a sheep or a dog*, she thought. And yet it didn't seem like either. It was moving too fast for a sheep and was too solid for a dog.

Shantih began to tremble. She made no attempt to run away but stood rooted to the track, shaking.

'Get on with you,' Jinny shouted, as much to encourage herself as to encourage Shantih. Whatever it was in the undergrowth was coming nearer. 'Walk on!'

Jinny caught a glimpse of a dark shape, a curved white tusk, a red-rimmed eye watching them. There was a grunting snort of fury and a black beast charged out of the bushes, straight at Shantih.

The Arab shied, throwing herself off the track to avoid the hurtling bulk. Jinny felt Shantih's hooves plunging into the mass of brambles, felt her fight to stay upright as the soft ground of the embankment gave way beneath her, and they fell.

Jinny was thrown out of the saddle, the reins plucked from her grasp as Shantih crashed down the side of the quarry, an uncontrollable mass of horse. At the bottom of the quarry she lay still.

Jinny threw herself down after her horse. She felt cold and detached. The need for immediate action took away all feeling.

In her fall, Shantih had trapped her hind legs under a heavy branch. Jinny tore at it. Lifted it a few inches, enough to let Shantih kick herself free. She snaked her neck and surged to her feet again.

Jinny snatched at her reins and led her round the enclosed space at the bottom of the quarry. She wasn't hurt. Sobbing with relief, Jinny collapsed on a block of stone, her legs fluid, her hands so worn out they could hardly hold the reins. She felt the hard lump in her anorak pocket. The statue was still there.

Jinny couldn't be certain, but she thought that the animal that had charged out of the bushes had been a black pig. The first time that Freda had come to Finmory she had said something about the boar being another of the Celts' sacred animals. But whatever it had been, it had not been a dream. It had been real enough to terrify Shantih. She could easily have broken her back in a fall like that. The power that had sent Jinny to find the statue of the Horse did not intend her to bury it back into the earth.

'Then what?' cried Jinny. 'What am I to do with it?'

Her words echoed round the quarry. She took the statue out of her pocket and stared down at the little Horse where it lay in the palm of her hand. It looked so alone. Jinny remembered how it had stood on the altar next to Epona.

Not one, said the voice in Jinny's head, the same voice that had spoken through her when she had stood in front of Epona in the Wilton Collection. *Not one, but* One.

And, all at once, Jinny knew what the voice meant, knew what she must do. Couldn't imagine why she hadn't known all along. She must take the Horse to Inverburgh to the Wilton to be with Epona. Leave the Horse there, beside Epona, as they had been on the altar. Then Epona would no longer be one alone. Together they would be whole, be One. This was why her dreams had led her to find the Horse; why *she* had found it and not the archaeologists who would have taken it away with them. This was what the Pony Folk wanted her to do for them.

'Tomorrow,' Jinny said aloud. 'First thing tomorrow morning I'll take the Horse back to Epona.'

Her words echoed round the quarry, seeming to reverberate into a deeper voice than her own.

The Horse with Epona. With Epona. The Horse with Epona.

And Jinny knew that she would have no more nightmares, would no longer be haunted by the brazen hoofbeats of the Red Horse. Now she knew what to do.

As Jinny led Shantih up out of the quarry, she felt as if a great weight had been lifted from her shoulders. She could breathe again, she could see again. She wasn't afraid anymore.

When she got out of the quarry, Jinny remounted and rode slowly back to Finmory. *I'll catch the first bus to Inverburgh*, she thought, then suddenly she knew

189

that she couldn't just go by bus to Inverburgh. It wouldn't be enough for the Horse. There should have been a procession, but Jinny couldn't manage that. The best she could do would be to ride Shantih to the Wilton.

'Ride to Inverburgh!' exclaimed Sue when Jinny asked her. 'Tomorrow morning?'

'I don't think I'd manage by myself. Shantih would behave herself better if she had Pippen beside her.'

'But why?' began Sue.

'I can't tell you now,' said Jinny. 'But I will, honest I will.'

Sue could tell from the state of Jinny's hair and clothes that she must have had a fall. Shantih, too, had bits of twigs clinging to her mane and tail, mud on her quarters, a long scratch on one of her white stockings. Yet Jinny seemed bubbling over with excitement, full of a secret that she couldn't share.

'Please,' said Jinny.

'All right,' said Sue.

Thirteen

It was very early in the morning when Jinny and Sue rode to Glenbost. The world about them was grey, without light.

'When we reach Glenbost we can go over the moor,' said Jinny. 'Over the top of the hills and down onto the Inverburgh road. Shouldn't think it's much quicker, but it cuts off a good bit of the road.'

Glenbost was still closed against the night, no lights showed in any of the croft windows. Mrs Simpson's shop was shuttered and dead. The junky, rusting cars piled outside the garage were in pools of deep shadow. A cat ran across the road in front of them, making Shantih drift sideways and Pippen prick his ears.

'Here,' said Jinny. 'It's this track, behind the church.' They left the road and began to climb into the hills.

The statue was in Jinny's pocket. Once she had

returned it to Epona, her part in the mystery would be over. Last night she had slept without dreaming. The Red Horse was satisfied. The mural on her wall was only a painting. She could not think why she had ever been afraid of it.

As they climbed, light seeped back into the world.

'Pretty steep here,' said Sue. 'Shall we lead them?'

'All right,' said Jinny dismounting.

Shantih walked sweetly at her side, mouthing the bit, her walk relaxed and easy.

This is how they brought them, thought Jinny. *Out of the darkness. The procession would be waiting down below to join them, but here in the hills the gods would be alone with the priestesses.*

They reached the crest of the hills. The Inverburgh road lay coiled beneath them.

'Whee!' exclaimed Sue. 'How about a breather?' She sat down on a comfortable rock.

Light from the rising sun arrowed across the moors. The rocks on the crest of the hills were rimmed with gold.

'Swear,' said Jinny to Sue. 'Swear on the thing you love most, your most precious thing, that you'll never tell anyone about what I'm going to show you.'

'Swear?' said Sue in amazement. 'What do you mean, swear? What are you going to show me?'

'Think of your mostest thing then say, "I swear,"' instructed Jinny.

Sue thought. 'I swear,' she said.

'Right,' said Jinny. She felt in her pocket and brought out the Horse. She set it on one of the rocks and it was ringed with the sun.

'What is it?'

'I found it at the dig,' said Jinny. 'It's a Celtic Horse god. It should be with Epona. Her statue is in the Wilton Collection and I'm taking it there.'

'Fancy you finding it! Didn't you tell them?'

'They wouldn't have given it to the Wilton,' said Jinny. 'That's why I found it, so I could take it to Epona.'

'It's an Arab,' said Sue. 'Couldn't be anything else. Maybe that's why you found it, because of Shantih being an Arab.'

They sat in silence, watching the Horse until the light spread over the sky and the Horse had lost its halo of sun.

'Are you just going to hand it to the curator at the Wilton?' asked Sue. 'Won't they want to know where you found it and all that?'

'I'll manage,' said Jinny, 'if you'll hold Shantih.'

'Do my best,' said Sue.

'Remember,' said Jinny, as she put the Horse back in her pocket, 'you swore.'

'To my grave,' said Sue.

When they reached the Inverburgh road it was already busy. A vast yellow lorry roared past, making Shantih rear.

'Single file,' said Sue. 'I'll go first. Pippen doesn't mind it.'

Keeping well into the side of the road, they made their way into Inverburgh. At first Jinny was tense, sitting stiffly, knowing that Shantih had never been ridden in traffic like this before; that if she got a fright and came down on the road she could break her knees, blemishing herself for life. A car transporter careered past, its twelve convict cars clanking behind it, and Shantih cantered on the spot, her shoes scoring the road.

If Pippen wasn't here she'd be away, thought Jinny, tugging frantically at Shantih's reins as she heard the rumble of another heavy lorry bearing down on them. 'Steady, Shantih, steady.'

The lorry roared past and Shantih shot forward into Pippen's broad rear.

'Oh, steady, you idiot,' cried Jinny. A bubble of panic blew up inside her head as she fought to control Shantih. Her elbow banged against the Horse in her pocket and suddenly Jinny remembered why she was there. They were taking the Horse back to Epona. She shouldn't be crawling along like this. The Horse must be at the head of the procession.

Jinny squared her shoulders, relaxed her stranglehold on Shantih's reins and sat down hard in the saddle. She rode alongside Sue.

'Shall we trot for a bit?' Jinny asked. 'I'll take Shantih

in front. She'll settle if she can trot out.'

Jinny let Shantih trot on, kept her moving forward, not letting her spook about.

'To take the Horse to Epona,' said Jinny aloud.

The traffic grew heavier as they reached Inverburgh, but still Jinny kept Shantih trotting, fleet and red-gold, she gallanted through the city din and fumes.

'Which way?' asked Sue at traffic lights.

'I know my way to Nell Storr's shop,' said Jinny. 'Once we're there it's only minutes to the Wilton.'

The lights changed to green and Jinny trotted on. Double-decker buses towered above them, motorbikes backfired, passengers in cars shouted and pointed, but Shantih paid no attention to any of them. She was all power and light, brilliant in the city grime. As she rode, Jinny was conscious of the Horse god in her pocket and of Epona waiting in her glass solitude.

If they could only see them, Jinny thought, looking down at the scurrying pedestrians from her horseman's pride. *Not as they will be in their glass case in the Wilton, but the way they were when the old woman sprinkled her herbs on the fire. If they could only see them. If they only knew what we are doing.*

They stopped outside Nell Storr's shop.

'Along this road,' said Jinny, leading the way to the Wilton.

When they turned into the road where the Wilton Collection was they seemed to drop into a silent well.

No traffic – even its noise was blown away over the high rooftops.

'About halfway down the road,' said Jinny, and, looking ahead, she saw the plaque on the door of the Wilton.

'Shall I just hold them in the street?' asked Sue doubtfully.

'Along there,' said Jinny, and they rode past the Wilton to where there was a rough patch of ground between two tenements.

'Even some grass for them,' said Jinny as she dismounted.

'Don't be too long,' warned Sue, taking Shantih's reins. 'I'll yell for you if I can't cope.'

Jinny hardly heard her. She took the Horse out of her pocket and held it in her hand.

'I shan't be long,' she said, and walked slowly up the road to the Wilton. She pushed the door open, went into the hall and stood at the bottom of the flight of stairs. There was no sound in the building, no noises from outside. Jinny climbed the stairs. The long corridor was empty. Carrying the Horse, she went quickly, silently, to the room where Epona waited.

Jinny paused in the doorway, swallowing hard, then crossed to the case in the corner. She moved as if she was flying – a lightness, a certainty. The lid of the case lifted easily. Epona waited, small and self-contained – expressionless. Very slowly, Jinny put the Horse down beside her as they had been on the altar.

'Together,' said Jinny, and, for a second, the vision flamed in her mind – the Horse in its awe and majesty, Epona with the fruit in her open hand.

Jinny closed the lid of the case, fitting the lock back into the rotting wood. When had the Horse and Epona last been seen together? Who had last seen them as she was seeing them now? Unanswerable questions built up in Jinny's mind.

Someone came into the room, came to stand beside Jinny. She looked up quickly, afraid they might have seen her. It was an old man, not much taller than Jinny, with a mane of thick grey hair, a brown suit and a gentleness about him.

He stood looking down at Epona and the Horse.

'You brought it?' he asked Jinny.

'Yes,' she said.

'He was right then, the man who brought Epona here. He said the Horse would follow.'

'Who brought Epona?' demanded Jinny.

'One of the travelling people. You can call them what you please. Some call them tinkers, some still use the old name – the Pony Folk.'

A cold shiver ran through Jinny. 'How did he know I would find the Horse?' she cried.

'He only said it would follow. He didn't mention you.'

'But it was me,' said Jinny. 'I dreamed the dreams.

197

I rode Shantih to Brachan back through time and saved the Horse from the archaeologists.'

'Enough that they are with each other again,' said the old man calmly. 'Tell me how it was.'

Standing, surrounded by objects, the Horse and Epona together in front of her, Jinny told him of her fears, her nightmares, her dream ride and how she had found the Horse.

The man nodded, understanding, accepting. 'We know so little,' he said. 'We are so lost that the gods must appear to us as beings of terror.' Then he turned, looking straight at Jinny, and said, 'Don't forget what has happened to you. Don't try and turn it into less than it is. Accept it as you accept the incredible miracle of food – apple blossom into apple.'

Jinny remembered Sue, left with Pippen and Shantih.

'I'll need to go,' she said awkwardly.

The old man nodded. He held out his hand to her. 'I'm Jo Wilton,' he said.'

'This is your museum?' exclaimed Jinny in surprise.

'Sanctuary,' said Jo Wilton and shook Jinny's hand. 'The Horse and Epona are safe here. When I die my grandson will take over. He knows far more than I do. My sons stood on my shoulders. My grandson stands on theirs. He was born knowing things I could never even reach. They will be safe with him.'

Jinny took one last look at the statues. They were together again. Her part was over.

'Goodbye,' she said, 'and thank you.'

'Thank *you*,' said Jo Wilton as Jinny ran out of the room.

She dashed along the corridor, hurtled down the stairs and half fell, half leaped into the open air.

'It's back,' she yelled to Sue. She wanted to sing and shout and dance. She was free again. Her face was spread in an enormous grin. 'I'm free! I'm free! I'm free!'

'Free or not,' said Sue. 'You have been ages. I thought Shantih was going to trample me underhoof.'

Still exploding with laughter, Jinny took Shantih's reins and mounted.

'Were they pleased you took the statue into them?'

Jinny considered the question as they rode along. Pleased was the wrong word. You weren't pleased about the air. It just was. The rightness of it was more than being pleased. 'It belonged there,' said Jinny at last.

They left the road and went over the hills to Glenbost. The sky blue, the air sharp. Jinny's mood was as high as the sky. Now there was nothing but light. Once Ken had said, 'it's all luminous Love', and, riding back over the hills to Glenbost, Jinny knew it was true.

She let Shantih sail over the stone walls, loving her speed and her courage. She loved Pippen, bustling behind her, loved his steadfastness, his placid contentment. She wanted to tell Sue how it was for her.

Kept saying to Sue, 'Isn't it wonderful. Isn't it all so wonderful.'

Glenbost lay huddled below them. As they rode down, the sun was high in cloudless blue sky.

'The day that Shantih escaped from the circus van was a day like this,' Jinny said. 'A blue day.'

For a moment, Jinny thought that the two days were linked. Shantih coming to Finmory so that she would be there to find the buried Horse god. But how could that possibly be? Jinny shook back her hair, laughing aloud, for it didn't matter. It was enough to be riding Shantih over the open land.

'Jump this bit,' Jinny called back to Sue, and cantered Shantih at a level bit of wall. Shantih leaped and landed in a smooth, flowing arc.

'Oh, horse!' cried Jinny. 'Oh, Shantih, Shantih, Shantih.'

They rode past the church and into the village. Dolina was standing outside the shop.

'You'll have been having the letter?' Dolina called, her face glum and despondent as she came across to them.

'What letter?' asked Jinny. But almost she knew. It couldn't have been any other way. She had always known that it couldn't happen.

'From the Education Committee. It's not the weekly boarding we're for. Haven't they found the dry rot in Duninver School? The whole floor's falling in on them.

They haven't the room for us. We're to be travelling to Inverburgh after all.'

'Well,' said Sue. 'Thank goodness for that.'

'Aren't you pleased?' she demanded, when Jinny said nothing, only sat on Shantih, staring at Dolina.

'I'll tell you this,' said Dolina. 'It's the better time we would have been having at the hostel. Clanging about in an old school bus all week. It's not me that would have been choosing that, I can tell you.'

Jinny hardly spoke all the way back to Finmory.

'I'm in shock,' she told Sue.

'See you tomorrow, then,' said Sue. 'When you've recovered.' And she turned Pippen to ride down to their tent.

'Yes,' said Jinny. 'Yes, OK.'

She couldn't start and thank Sue for riding with her to Inverburgh, not just now. She would do that tomorrow. Tomorrow would be cavalletti and the freedom of the moors, no longer haunted by the terror of hoofbeats, the presence of the Red Horse. But today Jinny was still caught up in the wonder that she didn't understand, could only live.

Ken had been waiting for her at the foot of the drive. He came from between the trees, Kelly shadowing his heels.

'You know,' he said, seeing Jinny's brightness. 'You've heard.'

'Yes,' said Jinny. 'I won't have to leave Shantih.

She won't have to go to Miss Tuke's.'

Saying the words aloud made it real. Jinny wanted to gallop and shout, send Shantih flying over the sands, soaring over the sun. All the things that had been closed against her were open now. Her new school, the Art Department, schooling Shantih, teaching her to jump, being able to speak to people again, not having to shut them out.

The Horse and Epona were together.

'Isn't it wonderful? Isn't it all so wonderful?' she demanded.

Ken laughed up at her. 'I keep on telling you,' he said. 'If you'd only listen.'

Editor's Note

Humans have been falling in love with horses for centuries – Jinny and Shantih, created in the 1970s are relative newcomers to the scene.

Here at Catnip we feel that this series was ahead of its time and is as fresh and relevant today as when it was first published. For this reason we have left Patricia Leitch's text in its original, startlingly beautiful, form.

Some of the cultural references reflect the time in which the books were written: a painting is sold for only two pounds whereas today it would be much more; top international showjumping contests are no longer held at Wembley. Yet the social issues and emotions tackled in each book are as timeless as the spiritual bond between girl and horse.

For Love of a Horse

Patricia Leitch

The horse was a pure-bred Arab. She came, bright and dancing, flaunting into the ring, her tail held high over her quarters, her silken mane flowing over the crest of her neck.

When Jinny Manders moves to the wilds of Finmory in the Scottish Highlands she has only one dream: a pony of her own. That's until a near-wild chestnut Arab steals her heart. But it seems the mare will never trust her, even though Jinny would risk everything to save the horse she loves.

A Devil to Ride

Patricia Leitch

Shantih bucked again; heels flung skywards, head and neck disappearing from in front of Jinny as she went soaring through the air, her long, straight, red-gold hair flying out behind her.

Worried that someone will discover that Shantih is too wild for her to ride, Jinny is desperate for help. When star showjumper Clare Burnley comes to the moors, Jinny thinks her prayers have been answered. But Clare's help comes at a price – one that Jinny seems only too willing to pay.

The Summer Riders

Patricia Leitch

'I'm just telling you,' Jinny said. 'Just so that you'll all know, that I don't think Marlene is fit to ride Shantih. I think she'll get hurt. And it won't be my fault when it happens.'

Town girl Marlene and her brother Bill have come to stay at Finmory, shattering Jinny's dreams of a summer spent riding Shantih over the moors. Now Jinny has to share her precious horse with someone she can't stand. But knowing nothing about horses doesn't mean Marlene can't teach Jinny a thing or two, as Jinny is about to find out.